ALL
THE WAYS
HOME

ALL THE WAYS HOME

ELSIE CHAPMAN

FEIWEL AND FRIENDS
NEW YORK

A Feiwel and Friends Book

An imprint of Macmillan Publishing Group, LLC

175 Fifth Avenue, New York, NY 10010

Our books may be purchased in bulk for promotional, educational, or business use. Please
contact your local bookseller or the Macmillan Corporate and Premium Sales Department
at (800) 221-7945 ext. 5442 or by email at MacmillanSpecialMarkets@macmillan.com.

Library of Congress Control Number: 2018955250

ISBN 978-1-250-16679-1 (hardcover) / ISBN 978-1-250-16678-4 (ebook)

Book design by Carol Ly

Feiwel and Friends logo designed by Filomena Tuosto

First edition, 2019

1 3 5 7 9 10 8 6 4 2

mackids.com

TO JESSE, MATTHEW, AND GILLIAN.
FOR ALL THE ADVENTURES.

1

The car is too hot and smells of leather, and my stomach dips up and down with it.

I think about unrolling the window some more but don't. My grandpa is talking to me as he drives, and it's an Important Talk. The sound of traffic coming from the freeway outside is already too loud, making him raise his voice. It makes him seem nearly angry, and I almost kind of wish he were, instead of disappointed. That's what he can't hide from creeping up into his eyes.

Mom inherited his eyes, and I know hers would have the same disappointment in them if she were here driving me instead. Except maybe ten times worse, since Grandpa is still a stranger, here for me now that there's no one else.

The airport is in Richmond, the suburb south of Vancouver, and still twenty minutes away. I slide down a bit farther in the passenger seat. My backpack is in my lap— inside is everything I'm going to need for the next three weeks, the last part of this strange and terrible summer. I'm about to fly over the ocean to a home I don't remember, and suddenly I'm sure I didn't pack enough. That I packed all the wrong things.

My grandpa clears his throat and adjusts a sleeve cuff, still driving.

He used to be a fancy accountant before retiring five years ago, but he continues to wear a suit every day, as though he's still going to work, complete with a tie and shiny loafers and everything. Mom said the habit's from when he first came to Canada from Japan with nothing but a wife, young daughter, and job skills that were no longer as good as they'd been on the other side of the ocean. Which means, I guess, that he's still scared of ever feeling that way again.

When I'm that old, I hope I'll be able to let go of stuff more easily.

Mom dying would be an example.

This mess I've gotten myself into might be another.

2

"Well, Kaede, don't forget to call once you land." My grandpa clears his throat again, like he's nervous around me, or unsure. Which I get because it's how I still feel around him. "Just so I know."

"It'll be like one in the morning Vancouver time." Tokyo is sixteen hours ahead, about as far away in the world as you can run. "I don't want to wake you up."

"Oh, right, the time difference. Leave a message, then, and you can call again once you're settled."

"Okay."

We've been living in the same house for months now, but he's just as stiff as he was back in the spring, when he first moved from his home in Ontario to come out west to be my legal guardian. We circle each other like animals in a too-small cage in the zoo, doing our best to not get in each other's way, but in each other's way anyway.

I guess it makes sense, him not enjoying the change. He'd never asked to become a parent again at his age, after already having his own life for years once he was done raising my mom. I think he does a lot of mental hand-wringing over it all, given how often I catch him watching me, a tired look in his eyes and his shoulders slumped.

I wish twelve wasn't considered too young to live by yourself. Seems it'd be easier all around. The only thing I can't do is drive, but I have my bike, and Grandpa could just make sure I always had enough in the bank for food. I'd email him my report cards so he'd know I was still going to school. Then he'd be able to move back to Ontario and be happy again doing all the things retired people like to do.

"Kaede? You haven't forgotten anything? You've packed all you need?"

"Nope, and yeah." I look out the window. We're going over the bridge that connects Vancouver to Richmond, the river below unable to decide between being blue or gray. The airport's close now.

"Did you go over the checklist one last time like I told you?"

"Yeah." It's not a long list. Just enough clothing to keep me going between loads of laundry at my dad's place in Tokyo. An emergency cash card from my grandpa I can use at an ATM. The lined spiral notebook I bought from the local Walmart for a journal.

It's buried now between the shirts and shorts and other clothes in my backpack, but still its corners dig into my legs through my shorts.

They're calling it the Summer Celebration Project, but I have different names for it, ones that feel real and remind me how important it actually is. Like the Journal of the Unknown, or the Book of Questions, or the Diary of Still

Figuring It Out—each of them are more truthful, more honest.

The project's supposed to save me.

It'd been the last day of school, five weeks ago back at the end of June, and we were each taking turns drawing from the hat Ms. Nanda held in her hand. It was a party one, one of those paper cones with the elastic around the bottom to go around your chin so it stays on your head. I remember thinking she must have chosen it to make the idea of home-work over the summer fun, but from the sounds of students complaining, I don't think it worked.

Someone in the back of the classroom began to moan like he was in pain.

Beside me, Gemma had dramatically thrown her head down onto her arms on the top of her desk.

And Jory, he would have turned from his seat near the front to make one of his awesomely ugly faces, holding it long enough that Ms. Nanda would finally have to tell him to quit it.

But Perry was sitting there instead, since Jory still wasn't back in school.

"Now listen, no switching topics with anyone else," Ms. Nanda had reminded us as we all went up and pulled out a piece of paper with a word written on it. "You can include journal entries, photos, drawings—anything you want that you think applies to your selected topic, as long as you can make it fit into a notebook. When school starts again in the fall, there will be a drop-off box set up outside of my office. After all your projects have been collected, they'll be put on display in the lobby in the glass case for the school to enjoy. Marks will count toward your next year's grades."

Some of the topics seemed way more fun than others. And safe.

Vacation.

Pets.

Food.

And some seemed anything *but* fun. Still safe, though.

Health.

Weather.

Transportation.

When it was my turn to pick, my chest went a bit tight as I read the word printed on the piece of paper.

Home.

Which might have been okay if it had been any other summer but this one. Because lately I have a lot more questions about home than I do answers, and I'm pretty sure Ms. Nanda won't want a notebook like that on display when it's supposed to be encouraging.

3

After all the topics had been sorted out and we'd double-checked our desks and the cloakroom to make sure nothing was left behind for the summer, Mr. Zaher called for me to see him in his office.

I didn't know what the school counselor wanted to talk about, only that it couldn't be good. The school year was nearly over, after all. My heart beat a little too loudly in my ears, and my feet moved like glacial blocks along the hall as I walked over. As a bonus, my stomach was hurting, too, as it'd started to lately whenever I worried a lot over something.

I already knew I probably wasn't going to pass Grade 7—I'd been letting everything slide since the spring. So I was already dreading the fall and watching all my friends walk into the junior high next door while I stayed behind in elementary, still a little kid who didn't know what he was doing. Now I was also dreading seeing that project display go up in the lobby.

Since I couldn't decide what would be more embarrassing—having my project included even though I'd failed or purposely left out *because* I'd failed—I decided I wasn't going to bother doing it at all.

There'd been a jar of Jelly Bellies on the table in the

office, and as Mr. Zaher talked, I slowly ate from it, slipping jelly beans into my mouth one by one.

Red Apple as he told me that the school knew about Mr. Ames and what I did to his house after my mom died in the spring.

Toasted Marshmallow as he said they'd been told about what I just did to Jory at hockey camp.

Piña Colada. He'd just been in touch with my grandpa, who told him how he'd arranged for me to visit my father and half brother in Japan in August, even though I hadn't seen either since moving to Vancouver with my mom when I was three and they'd stayed behind. My grandpa had confessed he was at a loss of what to do with me—it'd been a long time since he'd been a kid. He no longer knew what made us work, what made us do what we did. As though we were another species.

Berry Blue. He said I was on the verge of having to repeat Grade 7, just as I'd thought. Principal Li wished he could simply give me a pass because of my mom. And Mrs. Nanda said she wanted to take into account my doing pretty well in subjects like gym and art to make up for completely bailing out in ones like reading and math and science. But she just couldn't.

French Vanilla as Mr. Zaher recounted the dozens of notes in my school file, all from March onward. For helping Vincent TP the cars in the teachers' parking lot, for fooling around in way too many classes, for handing in essays I copied off ones I found online. Fistfights in the halls, too.

Chili Mango. I had too much potential to become the kind of kid I was becoming. So Mr. Zaher, Principal Li, and Mrs. Nanda got together and agreed that if I could do a good job on my Summer Celebration Project ("Not just average, not just all right, but a truly excellent effort, Kaede," Mr. Zaher had said as he poured more jelly beans into the bowl from a bag he kept in his desk), I would get to graduate. The mark would go toward this year's grade instead of next. With my grandpa's okay, the school was making me an exception, they said, waiting as long as they were. Making it be up to me.

So it was my final chance.

Do or die, all or nothing.

Watermelon.

Lemon Lime.

Caramel Corn.

I ate them all, one after another after another, as I digested this news. The sugar sat in my stomach like a lump and made it hurt even more. I knew I didn't have a choice now about figuring out what home meant to me, and it made me panicky inside, and desperate.

But despite everything, I wondered, What if it wasn't as hopeless as it seemed? What if it *wasn't* too late?

Sure, a lot of things depended on what I didn't know, on what I was still clueless about how to feel.

Things like finally seeing my long-absent father and brother (his name is Shoma) again and doing my best to pretend I was okay with being unwelcome.

Getting over my mom being gone and used to the idea of living with a relative who seemed perfectly set on staying distant.

Figuring out a way to convince my best friend to forgive me for taking away what he loves most.

And on top of all that, not failing Grade 7.

That was a lot of unknowns, yeah, and it had to fill an entire notebook.

But I had to start somewhere.

It might as well be halfway around the world.

"So what do you think?" Mr. Zaher's smile was a bit sad, as it was each time he saw me now, ever since the accident. I was pretty sure he didn't know it showed.

"I want to say yes, but is there any way I can choose another topic?" I didn't want any more jelly beans. I chewed my lip instead, nervous.

"What do you have?"

"Home. But I'll be in two different places this summer. I won't know what to write about."

Mr. Zaher smiled again, his eyes smiling along this time. "I'm sure you'll figure it out as you go, Kaede."

4

Dear Dad,

I'm on the plane right now, kilometers and hours and clouds zooming by. The sun coming in through the window bounces off the page of my open journal the same way it flashes off water, so everything's too bright and hard to look at.

Well, I'd *like* to blame the sun for making it hard to work, but I know it's really just me that's the problem.

I'm supposed to be writing about the topic of home for my project, but I haven't figured out how to start yet. I think I'm stuck because it can mean both big and small things, from a bedroom to a house to a city to a country, from a person to parents to a family. What if someone has all of that but still feels lost?

My teacher at school said one idea was to ask you about our family tree, that you and Mom getting divorced more than nine years ago wouldn't change you knowing. So even though it's been that long since we've seen each other—and three since we last spoke—I guess I have some home-work for you.

We're only a couple of hours from landing, and if I close my eyes I can pretend I'm still back in Vancouver, hanging out with Jory and Gemma, my best friends. We'd be heading to the Mac's two blocks away for slushies before biking over to the neighborhood park. There's a small basketball court there, and we usually just shoot pucks around the concrete until the high school kids come and chase us away.

I don't usually let myself pretend it's any time before the spring—before Mom died—because that's hard. So I pretend it's either April or May, somewhere in the months between Mom's accident and before I finally went too far at hockey camp, that period of time when sometimes I was angry before I even knew it, when that anger came out before I could stop it.

What I did to Mr. Ames was one of those times (even if a small part of me still wants to believe he deserved it).

Shoma would have filled in that part for you by now, just as he would have about my messing up in school and what happened with Jory. How it seemed I needed some time away, a change of scenery. Turns out you were away on a photo shoot when Grandpa tried to reach you to talk about my coming to visit and instead had to hunt down Shoma on his cell.

And Shoma would have been the one to tell you about Mom dying, too, because you hadn't been around to answer that call, either. I can't even remember where Shoma said you were, what you were away taking photos of. I just kept picturing our phone calls, these transparent sound waves making the leap from Canada all the way across the Pacific, only to keep falling into this black hole of a void over in

Japan, seven and a half thousand kilometers away. Those calls were like the blank end pieces of strips of negatives, or photos that dared to be out of focus—so you discarded them from the start.

It took us a while to find your number to make those calls. It was like following a broken trail of clues. You and Shoma moved around Tokyo a lot after me and Mom left for Vancouver, the city where she spent most of her childhood, where she wanted me to grow up, too. You guys moved from our place in Ikebukuro to Ueno to Kichijoji, and now you live in an apartment in Nakano while Shoma's old enough to be on his own in Shinjuku.

It wasn't long before the two of you were only as real as the characters I saw on TV, something someone imagined. And you never got older or bigger, just more faint, both of your outlines blurred. These days I remember almost nothing about you or Shoma or our old apartment in Ikebukuro.

Mom had let your latest number get buried beneath other contacts she somehow needed more often. The dry cleaner. Our dentist. A coworker from her old office I don't remember her ever talking about.

It was what I did to Mr. Ames and then to Jory (who actually didn't deserve it at all) that made Grandpa decide he already needed a break from parenting. I watched him call your cell again, over and over, like it was just a matter of will. Neither of us were really surprised when you never ended up answering. But Grandpa still looked at me as if it were my fault you weren't there, and I had to go get something from the fridge even though I wasn't hungry, just to hide how my face was hot and my eyes sore.

Because, see, for a second, it was Mom I saw, looking at me that way. It didn't happen a lot, but it accidentally slipped through sometimes—how she still wondered if I might have been the difference between you guys staying together or not. Or maybe she caught a glimpse of you in me and wasn't sure if she liked or hated that.

I think she had a lot of questions for you that she never ended up asking. You were never around to ask, and now she can't.

But I still can. Not ask her questions, but ones of my own that I guess I've been collecting over the years, wanting to know how you can be a ghost while still alive. Mine are sharp little rocks I keep in a small box, sort of like how my friend Donovan's mom keeps his little sister's baby teeth in a jar—each time there's a new one, she just places it on top. A mountain of teeth.

I feel weird about it now, thinking about how I kept trying to connect with you, sure the next time would be when you'd finally answer. Begging Mom to send you my drawings from school, then my report cards. The way I'd email you and how you started taking longer and longer between replies. Then no more birthday presents came in the mail after I turned seven, and no more phone calls or replies to those emails after I was nine.

It's not like you disappearing didn't get easier, though. It did. You being Dad faded until you became more like the *idea* of Dad. I got older and new memories got made, and Mom always did her best to be more than enough. Most of the time she was. She kept life busy so I wouldn't have time to peek into that small box of tough questions.

Now that she's gone, that box has been blown wide open. And there are sharp rocks everywhere I turn, ready to cut me.

I'm kind of tired of being surrounded by all of that, Dad. I don't really want to carry that small box around anymore, either, talking to me when I'm most lonely and able to catch me off guard.

But I might need some help packing up those sharp rocks and sending them away for good. Which means alongside the ones about our family tree, I've got some other questions I need to finally ask you.

Like was it really me and Mom not being enough and that's why you stopped bothering to try? Or was it just that Shoma by himself already was? Or that it was work you chose to let fill your head and heart instead?

I think being able to hear you say it in person will do the trick. I'll be able to take that small box full of those freshly packed-up rocks, and I'll imagine dropping the whole thing into the ocean on my way back home. I want to head into those waters on a sure and steady boat and let all those questions slip to the bottom and out of sight for good.

And then I'll know I'll be okay that you're gone.

Even when you're not.

5

One of the customs agents at Haneda Airport flips open my passport and asks me a question.

I stare at her, and my mind goes completely blank—I'm not used to anyone other than my mom speaking Japanese to me, with her own personal quirks and twists of the language. Even my grandpa speaks only English with me.

"Sorry?" I stammer out. My Japanese comes out creaky and full of cracks. It's been months since I've used it.

She smiles. "For how long are you staying in Japan?"

"Oh. Just three weeks." She starts to stamp pages inside my passport, and I glance at the fingerprint machine that's on the counter in front of me, at the digital eye scanner. The sign on the wall says they need to be used for visitors over the age of sixteen, how it's just a routine procedure in order to enter the country. But it doesn't keep my heart from starting to hammer, from my feeling like a criminal all over again the way I did that night.

The inside of the police car hadn't smelled like doughnuts or coffee, something I'd expected from movies. And there was no wire grate to protect the front seat from the back (I guess the cops saved the cars that had them for criminals older than twelve). But the police radio crackled with bursts of static just like it did in cop shows, and there were no door handles on the inside. And as the cops drove me away from Mr. Ames's house, I could still smell the smoke from the fire I'd set. Could still see the orange of the flames against my eyelids whenever I blinked. The sleeping streets were gray as they rolled by, and the moon shining over them was like an eye watching me. I had a stomachache the entire way home.

The customs agent hands me back my passport. She's still smiling because she doesn't know what I've done. She looks down at what I'd scrawled on the landing card—my dad's name and his address in the Nakano area in Tokyo. "And you have someone meeting you at the arrivals gate?"

"Um, yeah, him." I point to my printing on the card. "My dad."

"Well, welcome back to Japan, and enjoy your stay."

The *welcome back* part throws me for a second. "Thanks, I will," I finally manage. My voice goes up at the end, as though I'm asking a question instead of answering one. She calls for the next person in line, and I move away, wondering.

Vacations are meant to be escapes, but *some* must end up feeling more like traps. Because I'm supposed to end up saved by the time this trip is done, yet I already feel too lost to get there. How do you navigate through waters when you don't even know how to swim? What if you can swim, but something happens that you can't ever prepare for? Gemma has a friend whose older sister drowned, swimming her regular morning swim out at one of the beaches. She'd gotten hit by a cramp. It came out of the blue. She'd been alone. She'd left home thinking she'd get to go back again.

I shove my passport into my backpack. I get a glimpse of my journal that's inside, the still-new-looking cover. Only one entry so far about home, and it's a letter to my dad of all people.

Not what I expected.

I decide that to be fair, I'll wait until he's used to my being around again, when he sees how I'm not really in the way, before I ask him about being a ghost in my life.

I follow the arrows that point me toward the exit. Baggage pickup comes up, and since I only have my backpack that I carried on, I break off from the crowd and head toward arrivals. Vancouver and Canada begin to slip away, and Tokyo and Japan come to greet me.

Like the drink vending machines that line the walls. I'll have to tell my anime- and manga-obsessed friend Roan that they really do have a lot of them here, just like he said. I don't remember living here, but he asks me about Japan all the time anyway, as though my being Japanese means the answer's built into my blood, knowledge that somehow comes naturally. When instead, most of the time I think that part of me is almost like a mask, which slips on and off whenever it feels like it, whether I want it to or not.

The escalators are different in Japan. Using them is an organized thing, the left side for standing and the right for walking. No one butts in. No one seems impatient. The custom is weirdly calming, almost too simple to believe it actually works as smoothly as it does.

There are ads for food everywhere, and restaurants. But instead of Tim Hortons selling the Timbits and Honey Crullers I grew up with, it's Mister Donut with Pon de Rings and Frank Pies. And most sushi seems to be just the raw kind, with nothing close to B.C. or California rolls.

Ten times more people live in Tokyo than Vancouver, in about a fifth of the space—this means I'm surrounded by noise. Bunches of voices going up and down and sideways like amusement park rides. I make out the sharper, more pointed sounds of Chinese because of the Vancouver that's still in my ears, hear how they clash and ring against the milder swooshes of Japanese.

Gemma is Chinese, and she compares the language to Pop Rocks candy on her tongue, all little bangs and fizzles. Whenever her parents argue, those fizzles turn into explosions, full of color and noise. But she says me and my mom speaking Japanese makes her think of saltwater taffy melting in the sun, all smooth and liquid and even. *Both are so different, Kaede, it'd be hard to pick one forever. Who would want to pick between candy?*

Signs in both Japanese and English are everywhere, and there are ones in Chinese and Korean, too. There are also signs in languages I don't know. It's the airport, and airports are, I think, like slices of the world.

I filter out everything but the Japanese characters.

My mom's language, and what she made sure I learned, too.

Train.

Taxi.

Exit.

Entrance.

East, west, south, north.

In my head I'm little again and at the kitchen table, my mom's radio playing low on the counter as always. Over the noise of it she corrected the order of my strokes, the deliberate placement of them. She told me how adding or taking away just one or two can change a character's entire meaning. How on paper not much separates *rain* from *cloud* from *snow*, even though to me one means west coast wet, and one is puffs of white, and one makes me think of hot chocolate. Sometimes one of her favorite songs would come on the radio and she'd turn it up, singing along really badly so we'd both laugh. But once it was over she'd turn the radio low again, and it was back to work.

I used to like learning kanji from my mom, until I didn't. No one else I knew had to study more after school was done for the day, even when it was sunny and everyone was outside. No one else had to learn to write three new alphabets for a single language. No one else had a mom who printed out actual worksheets from the workbooks she brought home from the bookstore, telling her kid she was worried he would forget a part of himself.

After I got into hockey with Jory a couple of years ago and most of my spare time got sucked up with practice, Mom finally gave up. I didn't tell her I didn't love hockey as much as she thought I did. How it was Jory who'd discovered he could live at the rink and be perfectly happy, and how I was still there waiting to feel that, too. She recycled the worksheets, packed away the workbooks in a banker's box in her closet, and said it was okay as long as I never forgot the basics, at the very least. *Did you know language shapes your brain, Kaede, and not the other way around? That culture shapes it, too? They are like hands in dough, kneading away, building and creating something. Never forget this other half of you, which seems far away but isn't, not really.*

And I haven't.

Mountain.

Sun.

Month.

Money.

Kanji come at me from all directions, both super-basic ones I learned a long time ago and more complex ones that are newer, and I soak them up. My brain feels like it's stretching, like it's thirstier than it's ever been now that there's finally water in sight.

But there are also characters that take me longer to place, that I need to think about to recall. I picture that banker's box at home full of the Japanese I'd mostly turned away, how I told my mom I probably wouldn't ever need it because

I knew English and lived in Canada. And as I make my way through an airport full of people I don't know, I'm struck by a sudden blast of loneliness, of just how alone I am now.

Mom, you and me, that was the plan. You were always supposed to be there. I'm just a kid, and it's not fair that you're gone when there was never anyone else.

My eyes sting, and all the signs blur so they become meaningless. I could be anywhere, anyone, set adrift at sea like one of those mysterious trees sometimes found bobbing around in the water, and no one can figure out what shore it'd been uprooted from.

South Korea's only two hours away. Hong Kong, less than five. I could use my grandpa's emergency cash card and buy a ticket to anywhere where I don't have to be Kaede Hirano, grand mess-up at twelve years old.

But I'm here. For the next three weeks I'm kind of home again, and it's the strangest feeling in the world.

I sweep my arm across my eyes until I can see again. I take a deep breath, tighten the straps of my backpack around my shoulders, and walk through the arrivals gate.

To introduce myself to my dad.

6

Right away I realize I should have gotten a picture of him or something.

How else am I going to find my dad in a crowd of people who are all looking to meet someone? I haven't seen him since I was three — all I have to go by now are what images I might be able to find online by using the airport's free Wi-Fi.

Then I think about how he didn't ask for a new photo of *me* to make sure we didn't miss each other, and my chest gets tight.

Mom stopped sending him school photos of me when I was six and the envelope came back marked as "Moved" with no known forwarding address. I remember how her face had gone stiff, her eyes tight at the corners as she said that maybe next time we should wait for him to ask for pictures first.

As far as I know, he never did.

And kids — especially little ones — are formless, faceless blobs, like amoebas in petri dishes, floating around all happy and rounded and clueless. But once they get to twelve, time's gotten there, too, and they don't look the same anymore.

Dad should know this, too.

My insides clench as the room starts to empty and no

one's eyes land on me, filled with relief and excitement. I send a text to his number—*Hi, where are you? I'm at arrivals*—and walk over to the wall of vending machines to wait for a text back. The idea of the room emptying all the way so I'm the only one left leaves me cold and dizzy.

I'd been locked out of the house once, coming back from getting a slushie from Mac's with Jory. I'd forgotten my key, and Mom had run out to the store, not knowing I was headed home already. I'd been eight. The sky had gotten darker and the shadows deeper; nothing looked safe. I'd sat frozen on the porch, root beer slushie melting in the cup in my hands, too scared to go anywhere else. It was the first time I felt what it might be like to have nowhere to go.

What if Dad forgot when he was supposed to come get me?

What if he forgot I was coming at all?

What if he keeps on forgetting forever?

I scan the rows of drinks in the machines, not thirsty at all, and realize I don't have any yen yet—my money's still in Canadian dollars. I pat my pockets stupidly anyway before bending down to poke my fingers into the return slot of one of the machines. I do it without thinking, all automatic. I hear in my head my mom saying I used to do it all the time as a little kid, before she broke me of the habit.

I don't remember always doing it. I also don't know why I just did it right now.

Who knew a vending machine could turn time backward, could bring me closer to being three again, to a land I've long forgotten?

A hand comes from over my shoulder to hold something in front of my face. It's a large gold coin, about the size of a Canadian loonie.

Five hundred Japanese yen.

"Need some change for a drink?"

I look up at the voice and turn around to see a guy standing there.

Thin and tall, his arms lanky, all wrists and elbows and knuckles too big for their fingers. Tattoos snake out from beneath the sleeves of his white T-shirt. Earrings, little silver square studs. Skinny-ish black jeans, even though it's summer and hot enough for shorts. A worn-out messenger bag lies slung across his side. His black hair is streaked shades of blue, worn short in the back and along the sides but long enough in the front to lie messily over his forehead and get into his eyes.

His face is mine, except thirteen years older.

My brother grins.

"Hey, Kaede," Shoma says. "So how was the flight?"

7

His Japanese is slower than the customs agent's.

More chill, as Gemma would say.

Or maybe I'm already getting used to hearing it from different people. But as my brain tries to accept that he's actually here, it's what's missing that's making me stumble.

I stand up and look over his shoulder. He's taller than I thought he would be. "Hi, Shoma. Where's Dad?"

My brother shoves his hair off his forehead, and his grin turns hesitant. "He's sorry he couldn't come. He signed on for another photo shoot out of town, so it's just me."

I stare at Shoma, my stomach slowly curling up.

I'd imagined so many different ways of meeting my dad, and in each of them he's required to actually be present.

"He's not in Tokyo?" I hope I don't sound as stupid as I feel. Because I *do* feel that way, seeing as I'm here, just like he'd asked, which is what he said he was looking forward to. How he'd be right here, too, waiting to meet me again.

But all of that had come through Shoma, who'd passed on the invite on our dad's behalf after telling him about Mr. Ames and Jory and how I was messing up in school.

Between me and Dad and Shoma, talking to each other is more complicated than it's supposed to be.

And somewhere in all that broken communication, my dad decided I could wait a little longer.

"No, he had to go to Hokkaido." Shoma slips the five-hundred-yen coin he's been holding into the nearest vending machine and punches the button for a green tea. "Kind of near Sapporo, but more up in the mountains."

Sapporo is hours away by plane, more than a day's travel if you stick to trains. It's like northern B.C. to Vancouver, a place with its own feel and smells and things that make it different from the Lower Mainland. Winter snow sticks more often than not, and people have to plug in their cars at night so their engines don't freeze. People talk about hunting instead of being vegan. You can drive for twenty minutes and officially be beyond town limits.

Sapporo is so far from Tokyo.

"When is he supposed to get back?" I ask.

"Well, you're here for three weeks, so definitely before that. But I don't know when exactly, and reception's bad up there—I can't get through on his cell."

I glance down at mine and notice how my text to my dad hasn't been answered. Gone into the void of no response.

"Is he staying at a hotel?" Does my dad *like* staying in hotels? Does he feel as at home in them as he might in his apartment in Nakano? *More* at home, even? Everything is only a guess. That's what you have to do with strangers. You guess.

"Something like that." Shoma takes out the change from

the return slot and slips some of it back through and presses the button for another green tea. "Maybe it's a bed-and-breakfast? Remind me to look it up later."

I peer over my brother's shoulder again, like he might be joking, like our dad really just wants to surprise me by pretending to be late. I wait for a second for Shoma to suddenly remember that Dad just got his dates mixed up because of course he'd be here otherwise. But I know there aren't any jokes, and there are no mix-ups, and reality is the hollowness that's filled my throat.

Shoma passes me one of the green teas, and I take it so I can look at it instead of him. But then I think of something, so I have to meet his eyes anyway.

"So I'm going to be staying with you, then?" I've always lumped my brother and dad together—they're a team, just like me and my mom used to be a team. Coming here, I never thought about having to be with Shoma on my own. On his own, he somehow seems even more of a stranger. Someone completely new.

"Yeah, if that's okay with you." My brother gives me another smile, and it looks real enough, and I tell myself he's not already tired of me. How it won't matter because I'll be tired of him first. His blue hair glows and his black jeans are ripped just so, and I tell myself it won't bother me if he gets bored. "I have to work, but you can still hang out with me. And I have an extra room in my apartment, so you'll be fine until Dad gets back. Sound good?"

I nod, not really sure at all.

8

After we exchange my Canadian dollars for yen at a kiosk and pick up a SIM card for my cell so I can stay online, we leave the airport for Shoma's place. Shinjuku is one of Tokyo's most crowded areas, and it's a couple of trains and transfers away.

Our car on the first train is pretty full, standing-room only. We hold on to hand straps suspended from the ceiling. The ground rumbles beneath my feet, kilometers of steel track being fed into shiny wheels. Commercials and train announcements play on the video screen above the doors—for upcoming stops, the arrival of a new summer tea, the takeout bento lunches always conveniently available from any local 7-Eleven.

Along the way, Shoma points out stuff through the windows. Sites that are in guidebooks, places that are in famous anime or manga or movies, touristy stuff I might want to check out before I have to leave. There are buildings both tall and short, their roofs sharp and modern and scraping at the sky, or dipping low and tiled a shiny blue, brown, gray. Their sides are concrete and wrapped with billboards and digital screens; they are brick and wood and covered with lines of laundry hung to dry. Balconies are stuffed with bikes and AC units and container plants. There are parks and shopping arcades and roads full of cars and buses and people. There are other trains careening down other tracks, going in all directions. Nothing is motionless, and everything is fast, fast, fast. It all feels not quite real.

Shoma keeps his voice low, but it's still the loudest thing around aside from the announcements playing on the screens. No one else in our car—or in any of the cars, I'd peered down the snaking line of them to check—talks; everyone's looking at their phone or reading or sleeping. Except Shoma doesn't seem to care. Or maybe he does, but he's decided silence between us is even more awkward than playing tourist guide.

But I'm only half listening, also busy watching dozing passengers somehow wake instantly at their stop. Maybe living here you slowly grow a sixth sense for time, for how much space you can take up in a super-crowded country and still be polite, for the best and most natural order of things to keep everything running smoothly.

If my mom had never left Japan, she wouldn't have been driving on that Canadian road at that moment, coming home to surprise me with doughnuts for breakfast.

If Mr. Ames had some of that sixth sense, he wouldn't have taken his eyes off the road to look at his cell phone. He would have seen the light change in time, seen my mom's car.

If my dad hadn't chosen work over us, then maybe none of this would be happening.

Enough *ifs* to fill a whole new box, and maybe it'd be

about the same size as the one I've already got that's filled with hard questions.

I peer out the train window, where the world's turned into a strange, unidentifiable blur. Parts of me feel the same way, cut loose to drift around and wander, maybe forever. Vancouver was home because it was where my mom was, just as much as Tokyo never was because that was where Dad and Shoma were.

The trip to Shinjuku takes us nearly an hour, the way the trains and transfers spread out into a bunch of different lines. Vancouver has the SkyTrain, but it would be a tiny corner of just one of the dozen or so transit maps that exist here. Shoma must be able to read my confusion because he says I'll get used to it soon enough. That once I figure it out, I can get practically anywhere in Tokyo without having to drive.

Shoma asks me stuff. Stuff he seems to know is safe.

Is the sushi in Vancouver as he good as he hears it is?

Is the rain as bad?

Have I seen much of the rest of Canada?

He doesn't ask me about Mom (other than to say he's sorry), or Jory, or Mr. Ames, or even how things are going at school. Like he's being as careful about my sorest spots as I am.

I ask him what he does for a job before he decides to stop being so careful.

"I'm a writer," he says. "Freelancer mostly. I write articles and do interviews for music magazines."

Music. I think of Mom and her constant radio before I

make myself stop, not ready to share that. "Like, album reviews and interviews with bands?"

Shoma nods. "I do write-ups about lives, too. So if I'm covering a tour for a special feature, it means getting paid to travel across the country."

I frown, confused. *Lives*, rhyming with *hives*. "What are 'lives'?"

"Oh, sorry. Concerts. That's what they're called here. Lives."

"Your job sounds pretty cool." I remember now, Mom telling me Shoma liked to write. When she used to talk about him sometimes, a long time ago, his name just popping up out of the blue like she couldn't help the memories from surfacing. *Your brother wanted a dog. Shoma used to write for his school paper. He would have liked this Chinese restaurant, this color of sweater.* But she eventually learned to stop, just like she stopped talking about Dad.

"It *is* cool, getting to write about music and being paid for it," Shoma agrees, smiling.

I can't miss his happiness with his work. Writing's stuck with him, then. The same way photography stuck for our dad, which he started when Shoma was just a little kid.

I wonder how much *Dad* stuck with my brother. What had he been like as a dad before I came along? Did his distance come from somewhere inside himself, something no kid could keep away? Or was it something else entirely, something a kid *still* wouldn't have a chance at beating? Was it anything a kid could even see coming?

Those tough questions in that small box—I hadn't known any of them could be for Shoma.

"Your Japanese is really good," my brother says as we get out at Shinagawa Station to transfer to the Yamanote Line. "I guess your mom spoke it with you at home?"

"Yeah, she was always worried I'd begin to forget it once I started going to school." It's odd talking about my mom to Shoma, even though for three years, she'd been his mom, too, the stepmom in his life from when he was twelve until he was nearly sixteen. Before the divorce happened, and he disappeared with our dad and she disappeared with me, his half brother.

"I wish my English was as good, at least good enough so we could speak to each other in it. But I only know a few words, and most of them are swear words." Shoma laughs. "Likely not the kind of conversation your mom would have wanted us to have." He scans his Suica fare card over the scanner at the gate, and the turnstile ushers him through.

My new Suica is shiny and slippery in my hand as I fumble it over the scanner. I nearly drop it. People are starting to pile up behind me, wanting to go through, too.

Shoma's put ten thousand yen on it, about a hundred Canadian dollars. His treat, he said—so his little brother could hang out and explore the city and still have enough to always get back.

A part of my brain had squeaked like a door hinge gone crooked when I saw Shoma punch in the amount at the fare machine. I thought of that money and how it would help pay for a plane ticket to Sapporo. About how maybe it made more sense to use it to go find my dad on my own (I'm twelve, allowed to fly alone here) instead of just waiting around for him to show. Shoma wouldn't know as much about our family tree, anyway, and I doubted he'd cheered when he'd been told about having to babysit. Then I watched Shoma feed bills into the machine and felt too guilty to think about it anymore.

"Kaede? You okay with the Suica?" Shoma's waiting for me on the other side of the gate. His blue hair stands out rebelliously, as loud as fresh paint, but his face says he's worried for me, looking a bit like a parent's. "Try it again."

I hold the card more carefully over the scanner and this time the turnstile moves. I walk through and follow Shoma down a flight of stairs and along the platform.

"How's your grandpa?" he asks as we stand in line and wait for the train. "You like living with him all right?"

I picture breakfast the morning I left—my bowl of Apple Cinnamon Cheerios and glass of orange juice, his black coffee and dry toast. The drone of the morning news coming from Mom's radio on the counter was the only real noise in the kitchen. (Grandpa never listens to anything else, not even sports radio. I haven't heard any of Mom's songs since she died, like they no longer exist just as she doesn't.) I don't really like cinnamon anything, but Grandpa can't seem to remember that, so he keeps buying it. I waited until he left the room before pouring the cereal still left in my bowl down the sink, before changing the radio station from news to music. The song wasn't one of Mom's favorites, but it was still one that I recognized. So I'd stood there, shoving my dishes into the dishwasher, eyes blurred because things nearly felt close to before.

"It's okay, I guess," I say to Shoma now. "It's still kind of weird, someone other than Mom living in the house. But I think it's getting better."

"Yeah?" My brother looks more closely at me. For a second it's like he wants to hear something else, maybe something closer to the truth. For a second, I wish I could spill and tell him everything.

Which doesn't really make sense because why would any of it matter to him? Our dad's coming back to Tokyo to pick me up, and then Shoma won't have to babysit me anymore and soon he'll forget I was even here. And then I'll be on a plane flying back over the ocean, to a house that now feels unfamiliar. Back to Jory and Mr. Ames and school.

My stomach tightens up into a knot, its ends thin and frayed. I just nod. "Yeah."

Then the train arrives, and we both push our way on. We pull away from the platform and the station, and I try to forget that second of nearly slipping. When, for that single second, it was almost like not being alone anymore.

9

Wiki tells me Shinjuku Station is the busiest in the world.

I want to tell Wiki that the word *busiest* kind of feels like an understatement.

We had a beehive at the house once, hanging from the banister of our back steps. At first it was just a tiny gray thing, about the size of my hand. Then seemingly overnight it blew up to the size of a basketball. The thing vibrated and thrummed, a motor encased in soft gray silk. Inside I knew there would be a map of a self-contained world, full of roads and paths and connected tunnels. It was neat to watch that world hum, the sound of it a low buzz in the air, even though it was also kind of scary. How did the bees keep from getting lost? How did they always know which way to go? What if instinct failed them and they just got stuck forever? Mom eventually called in pest control, and the guy smoked it all into silence. We were safe from stings then.

Afterward me and Jory and Gemma had poked it halfway open with a stick before we decided to stop. It'd felt wrong, somehow. Like we were dissecting something still living, a body that still clung to a soul. Those bees were gone, but still they'd left signs behind that they'd been real. That they'd existed, had found places of their own somewhere in all those tunnels.

Shinjuku Station makes me think of that nest now, with its tangle of gates and hallways, its fast-walking passengers who all have somewhere to go. It makes me think of a human heart, too. How it's full of veins and arteries just pumping life along all its paths. So when a train arrives and pours out even more people, that's the rush of your pulse in your ears, the steady whoosh of it telling you you're alive.

Navigating our way through the station, I decide three things about Shoma that are as indisputable as fact.

One. My brother is cool, really cool. Not just because he's got blue hair and writes about rock concerts and hasn't said anything that comes close to being weird or creepy, but because he doesn't even care that he is. (Cool, that is, not creepy.)

Two. My brother has to be just like my dad, his tag-team partner—Shoma hadn't been any better at being around, either. And he's only babysitting me because he couldn't get out of it. So if I'm even close to being smart, I should do my best to not like him.

Three. Number one is going to make sticking to number two pretty hard.

We step outside, and Tokyo's boiling.

I stop dead in my tracks as a wall of heat smacks me right in the face. The air is almost wet, like rain caught halfway.

"Why is it so hard to breathe?" I manage. "Is this normal?"

Shoma laughs and slips on sunglasses he pulls out from

his pocket. "Yeah, August in Tokyo can be pretty deadly. You'll get used to it."

I wonder how long it'll be before that happens. Before Japan gets into my blood and changes me from the inside out. In three weeks, will I be more like Shoma, confident behind his glasses and easy with who he is? Or more like Kaede than ever, heading back still complete with questions?

"You hungry?" Shoma asks.

"Kind of? I'm too hot to tell."

"There's a great noodle place a few blocks over that serves them cold. And it's on the way to my place. Let's go."

My eyes are everywhere as we walk. It's impossible to take it all in, but I try anyway, dodging incoming waves of people along the sidewalk. Shinjuku is noise and color, and it's like trying to slow down a firecracker to keep it from going off in your hand.

Shoma points out the direction of Koreatown, a ten-minute walk away toward Okubo, the next station over; the skyscraper district in the west, its buildings all huge, silver teeth; Kabukicho, an area too seedy for me to explore on my own. *Especially at night, Kaede.*

Different scents roll out from the restaurants we pass: fishy, all salt and brine and smelling of the sea; smoky, mysterious tea; red bean paste for dessert, turned stiff with sugar. There's an arcade with taiko drums and photo booths. A café sells French-style crepes with whole wedges of cake rolled up inside. An old lady sits behind the window of a kiosk, smoking and reading and selling cigarettes and magazines. A store with racks of T-shirts and pullovers on the sidewalk, all with English sayings printed on the front. *California Dreaming. Elvis Loves Peanut Butter. Washington University.*

Shoma stops in front of a dark-walled shop. There's a food ticket machine just outside the main door, its menu rows of lit-up buttons. Shoma pays for us both—"Food's on me while you're in town, just don't expect fancy ten-course kaiseki meals, okay?"—and shoves in a bill and a bunch of coins. The machine spits out tickets, and we go inside the restaurant.

The air-conditioning is on, but it's still only just a bit cooler than out on the street. The whole place smells of soft flour and fresh noodles and cooking broth, of things made to fill up emptiness.

I guess, maybe, that I'm hungry after all.

10

The food comes quick, served to us at the counter where we're sitting. I do my best to slurp my noodles, the way you're supposed to eat them here, but it's hard to instantly unlearn nine years of *not* doing that.

"So what's on your list of tourist things to see and do?" Shoma slides negi into his dipping broth. The slices of green onion float for a second before he stirs them down with a dab of wasabi. Once, as really little kids, I'd convinced Jory the green stuff was pistachio ice cream. He'd eaten a whole spoonful in one go. He wheezed so hard and went so red that I got scared and started crying. And then *he* started crying seeing me because he thought it meant he was really going to die. Mom grounded me for two weeks, and after I was allowed to go out again, she made me treat Jory to ice cream for real. "I have some lives I have to cover, but otherwise I'm game for whatever you feel like."

"I can read enough Japanese that I can get around on my own." It'll be simpler this way, I tell myself, doing stuff alone. I need to climb on that boat with that box of tough questions and just sail through until I can get to Dad. No distractions, no detours. No brothers too easy to like.

"Your mom would kill me if I let you do that." Shoma refills our glasses with cold tea from the pitcher on the counter. "Don't make me stalk you around Tokyo, dude." He says this easily, casually. But his voice has gone quiet at the mention of Mom. Thin and uneven, too, the way a sprained ankle might sound if it could talk.

"You can't know how Mom would feel about me doing that," I say, confused. How much can Shoma remember about my mom? Sure, he'd already been fifteen when we moved away, but it was still more than nine years ago. "You barely knew her."

"Sure I knew her. She was my mom, too, for three years. And she'd definitely want me watching out for you while you're here. If you need ideas for places, just ask. Ideas can't hurt, right?"

His voice is still kind of odd sounding, and I remind myself that my mom had once loved him, had loved him as much as me. And for the first time it sinks in that he's lost not just one mom, but *two*, and it's weird to suddenly feel sorry for my super-cool older brother.

Maybe . . . maybe it's okay to want Shoma to stop being so much of a question, too.

Through a mouth of half-chewed noodles I slowly tell him about my Summer Celebration Project. "If I do a really good job, I can start Grade 8 next year with my friends instead of staying back." The idea of failing Grade 7 is bigger than just being left behind. Failing means being known the whole year as the kid with the dead mom, who set a guy's house on fire, who sent his best friend to the hospital. Who belongs nowhere.

"So that might be fun, right?" Shoma asks. "Like some kind of travel diary, except with a theme."

I nod. "My theme's home."

"They couldn't give you a break about your grades, considering your mom?"

"I got into some fights, too. Pulled some dumb jokes on the teachers."

Shoma laughs. "You don't look like the delinquent type, Kaede. What were you thinking?"

"I guess I wasn't."

"And that's on top of what happened to your friend, him getting hurt at hockey camp." Shoma doesn't look at me as he talks, like he somehow knows not to. He doesn't point out how *I'm* what happened to Jory, and why he's still hurt.

My brother isn't supposed to be nice.

I slowly stir my noodles with a chopstick, no longer hungry. "Yup."

For a moment, we don't say anything. He drinks tea, and I just keep stirring. There's a game show on the TV mounted on the wall, the wacky kind Japan can be known for. In this one, the loser has to strip to his boxers before getting a foam bat across the face. We're both watching without watching.

"Kaede, do you know the word *kotodama*?" Shoma asks.

I shake my head. If Mom had taught me that one, I'd forgotten.

"The kanji for *koto* means 'to say' and the one for *dama*

means 'spirit' or 'soul.' Put together, *kotodama* means 'the power of words.'"

I shake my head again. I know each kanji on its own—they're basics and form lots of words with other kanji—but this combination is new to me.

"It's from old Japanese mythology. If you watch enough anime or read enough manga, you'll probably come across characters whose special abilities come from the power of words." Shoma gives me a crooked smile, now looking unsure of bringing it up. "Anyway. I'm just thinking about your journal and how it seems you're being asked to write your way through this."

"The way you might? With work?"

"Sure. I mean, some articles *are* harder to write, but I still have to write them."

I think of my mostly blank journal, in my bag on the shelf beneath the counter. How, over three weeks, writing will help me change all the questions in my head into answers.

I wonder if that's why Shoma writes. If he had to work his way through stuff, too, to end up where he is now. Dad's itchy feet didn't get bad until after me and Mom were around, but he started getting into photography soon after Shoma's mom died, when Shoma was eight. Whatever the reason for our dad being distant, maybe Shoma's house when he'd been a kid had been empty in weird ways, too.

"And, Kaede, about the driver of the other car, the one from the accident . . ." My brother gives me a look so gentle my eyes prickle. "The way you tried to set his house on fire—

you're lucky it didn't end up worse than it was, you know? He could have made the police be harder on you, you being twelve or not."

I go stiff. My heart pounds. Disappointing Shoma had never been a thought, and now it feels like it matters too much. A part of me wants to erase my brother back into an outline, back into the distance, where I can keep him small. Another part wants to paint him true, let his blue hair be a blaze.

"I wanted the police to make it harder on *him*," I say. "For what he did."

"But you know the difference between negligence and intent, right?"

I do. It's about being careless instead of being on purpose. Everyone kept telling me, and I hadn't cared. I still don't want to now, even if I do understand it better.

"I said this to your grandpa on the phone after I heard about the accident," he says slowly, "but really it's you I should have said it to. Kaede, I'm sorry again about what happened to your mom. She was always good to me, when she could have easily chosen not to be. There I was, this brand-new twelve-year-old kid she was suddenly expected to treat like her own, and she did. For three years I was hers, and I had a family again."

My brother's voice has gone funny once more, full of gaps and broken up like a fence that needs repair. Still, the expression in his eyes somehow reminds me of my mom's, those times she looked at me and I knew she would somehow make things right. Cooking my favorite dinners on Father's Day, extra birthday presents for the ones that stopped coming in the mail. *Not to make up for your dad not being around, Kaede, but because I am.*

"You about done?" Shoma pushes away his tray. "Home is just a ten-minute walk from here."

My mom had once loved him, yeah.

And I know I must have, too.

11

I used to google my dad sometimes, back when I still let myself miss him.

Tsubasa Hirano is a pretty big photographer in Japan now. After me and Mom moved away, he was finally able to really focus on building his career. And Shoma was already a teenager by then, so family was no longer a worry or a care. His name began to mean something when it came to galleries and art showings and studios. People wanted their share of him. On paper, on a computer screen, he felt more and more like a stranger and less like my dad.

He does mostly landscapes and buildings and street scenes.

Together, those three things have taken him around the world, to places far away from us. But it's like he leaves a piece of himself behind each time, wherever each photo shoot takes him. So when he comes back to Japan, not all of him is here anymore. I think it's kind of the same way with Jory and how he lives at the rink as much as he can. When he's away from it, he can't hide he's missing something.

The difference is, Jory's found his home at the rink and is happy there — my dad's happiness comes from the search.

I found this one online interview three years ago; the publication date was one year earlier.

Reading it, I'd been so proud of him, how he sounded like a celebrity the way he touched so many people with his photos—*That's my dad! That's his work!* But afterward, my stomach was shaky, all hollowed out. As though his answers to the interviewer's questions had opened up these cracks inside me, and all my pride was seeping into them even as other things leaked out.

I had questions.

Like why did my dad's search for satisfaction have to take him away instead of bringing him closer?

Why did the people he most wanted to make happy with his photos seem to be everyone but family?

Why didn't his being my dad mean most of him wasn't for sharing?

I'd been nine when I read that interview.

It'd been nearly a year since I last heard from him.

This part is the worst:

"I'll never stop looking for new places. It's the best way I know how to keep feeling inspired, to stay feeling young."

Does Hirano think he has more than just a slight case of wanderlust?

Another laugh. "Home is . . . complicated, that's for sure. I can't deny that for me, personally, the concept of home often feels more stifling than comforting. On occasion, when a location is particularly tough, there will be a moment or two where I think feeling that way is more a curse than a blessing. But then the light turns just right, and I manage to capture something special in a photo. And I remember all over again why I'm there—why I do what I do, no matter the cost."

12

The name of the all-night café Shoma lives upstairs from is Irusu. It means "pretending to not be home," which is kind of perfect for a place that never closes, always there for those who need somewhere to be. I would wonder about his sleeping because of noise from the café at night, but noise—*music*—is his life, so it works out all right.

Rows of plastic food line the front display window, shiny in the late afternoon sun: omurice, mixed sandwiches, doria. Past them I see leather booths, wood floors, brass lamps, a clerk at the till by the entrance. There's a second floor, too, Shoma tells me, with more booths and a walled-off smoking section that still lets smoke billow everywhere.

I follow him as he navigates the tiny path between the café and the building next door, an acupuncture clinic. The slabs of pavement are uneven beneath my steps, and cracked. But someone's kept them swept. The weeds have been cut back and thrown away. There aren't any cigarette butts, smoking section or not.

There's a door at the back of the café building. A planter of bright-yellow flowers sits beside it. Beside that, there's a small white lucky cat figurine, its paw raised. It's the motion-sensitive kind, so it waves its paw as we get close. A bunch of five-yen coins lay scattered at its feet. The five-yen coin is supposed to be the most important one when it comes to praying. I remember my mom telling me it's because it's pronounced the same way *good luck* is in Japanese. Looking at them, I wonder if any are Shoma's, from when he might have wanted something, or had something to wish for.

My brother unlocks the door, and inside we start climbing the stairs. Three steep flights—his rental apartment is on the top floor. The walls are close, the light dim—the banister is cold beneath my hand.

"Shoma, you know those old Japanese horror movies?" I'm practically whispering, but I can't help it. "Like *The Ring* and *The Grudge*?"

He laughs. The sound echoes. It's kind of cool—that I can make him laugh, despite his being so much older, his experience in so much. "Yeah, why?"

"Just asking."

Another laugh as he fishes out a second key once we get to his front door. He's already given me a spare set for both doors. *For when you're out on your own and want to come home.*

"Are you talking about the Hollywood versions or the real thing?" he asks.

"Hollywood. I've never seen the originals."

"Seriously? Okay, add that to your list of things to do. 'While in Japan: define the concept of home and learn the source material.'"

Shoma's place is pocket-sized—two bedrooms, a bathroom, and the tiniest kitchen and front room I've ever seen, all fitting into a space that's about half the size of our house at home. Seeing it reminds me of something Gemma had told me, after I told her where I was spending August and she'd gone online to read about Tokyo. *Did you know Japan is around the same size as California? But while thirty-nine million people live in California,* one hundred and twenty-seven million *people live in Japan?*

The bedroom that's mine until I get to Dad's is a tiny corner of that pocket. The floor is covered with tatami mats that smell like grass. The walls are covered with white paper with the texture of woven fabric. My Western-raised feet appear oversized on the mats, my fingers clumsy and careless as I stretch out, nearly able to touch opposite sides of the room at the same time. Then I stop and drop my arms, wary of all the shelves and racks just at my fingertips. There's not enough buffer room between me and this space that's not mine—I don't want to damage something. Or have something damage me.

I drop my backpack onto the tiny futon left out on the floor and carefully look around at my brother's stuff.

There's a bookshelf shoved full of old manga and music magazines. Vinyl records are stacked on top of a turntable on the floor, and there's a plastic yellow crate full of CDs beside that. A bin is full of anime figures still in plastic bags, ones from *Naruto, One Piece, Bleach.* Roan would be in heaven if he could see, and I grin to myself. Shoma doesn't really seem like an anime geek, but that's the foreigner in me talking. We read and see things and decide what is normal, when really we can't know much at all. Coming here and observing doesn't mean I suddenly understand.

I have to admit I like seeing how my brother is also a collector, though. Just like me. One more way we're alike, outside of having the same dad. I keep limited edition quarters and hockey cards; he keeps CDs and magazines. This spare bedroom of his feels about five times smaller than my room in Vancouver, but it doesn't seem to have stopped Shoma much.

If I'd had such little space growing up, would I have bothered to keep anything? If Shoma had had my room, would he have gone wild and brought the world home, saved it as his own? If I'd grown up here, would I still be the kind of person who could hurt his best friend? Would Shoma be a writer if he lived in Vancouver? Maybe we'd just be more like each other, or different in ways that aren't so big.

I open the closet door, shaking the questions away—I won't be around long enough for the answers to matter.

Jackets are stuffed along a rail. There are shoe boxes lying on the floor. Behind all of this, partially hidden, are an electric guitar and a small amp. Both look like they've been used a lot, and that they'd been expensive, but I can't tell for sure. And then that corner of my brain squeaks again, and I'm thinking about that plane ticket to Sapporo and how it can't be cheap. I'm thinking how Shinjuku is a city that dwarfs Vancouver—and even Vancouver has its share of resale shops.

Guilt burns my ears, and I back away, shutting the closet door with click.

There's a knock, and it's Shoma, standing in the hall just outside the room.

"Hey, you okay in here?" he asks. "Sorry about the mess. You can just shove everything around if you like."

"I'm fine." My answer half surprises me, because it's mostly true. Shoma's hiding how much he hates having to babysit, and if I'm careful, he'll stay a stranger. The next three weeks might not be as bad as I once thought, with only a missing Dad left to solve on this side of the ocean.

Only.

Relief instantly turns into dread. The sharp lump of it sits in my throat.

Meeting my dad has become a waiting game now, when all along I'd meant to get it over with. That box of tough questions is getting heavier. My boat will sink if I let leaks take over—if I wait too long out on the water.

And Shoma—can't he see he's only making it harder, pretending to care? He's been gone for nine years with barely a word, and nine years is kind of a long time when I think about how long some school days can feel. People sometimes think rebooting a computer that's crashed is simple, just a flick of a switch and everything's back the way it was. But programs get wiped out. Work gets lost. It can get really messy. Some of it might not be recoverable.

You can't become brothers overnight.

"I just realized you should probably call your grandpa, now that you're here," Shoma says, still standing in the doorway. "It's the middle of the night in Vancouver, so he'll probably be asleep, but . . ."

I'd forgotten, and I feel guiltier about it than I thought I would. Which is weird because I'd only be calling to speak to a machine, while Grandpa and I barely speak even when we're face-to-face. "It's okay, he told me to just leave a message this time. I'll call in a second."

"Okay, sounds good. And you should try to stay up for a bit longer, or it'll be harder to get over the jet lag. How about call home, finish unpacking, and then we'll head out again?"

"What would we do?" It's nearly seven in the evening here, but back in Vancouver I'd be sleeping, just like Grandpa is sleeping now. I'd be having bad dreams about fires or car crashes or hockey accidents. The house would be dead quiet all around me, most of the city just as quiet.

My brother shrugs, gives me a grin. "It's Tokyo, Kaede, and we're in Shinjuku—there's going to be something. And there's always food, too—dessert, if you want. I bet you can't get good taiyaki in Vancouver. Or kakigori."

It takes me a few seconds to connect the words to the right food. Taiyaki: fish-shaped pastry filled with bean paste, sometimes with shiratama, too. The World Food Day fair has them, but that's only once a year, and they probably can't compare. Kakigori is shaved ice Japanese style. A store in a mall in Burnaby claims to sell them, but they ended up being more like American snow cones, the ice in hard crystals instead of soft flakes, the flavoring brightly colored sugar syrups you squeeze from a bottle instead of fruit and condensed milk ladled on top.

Shoma's still waiting for an answer by the time I'm done thinking all this, and I stare up at him, uncertain. The idea of seeing Shinjuku at night—it's just going to be another memory I'll regret. Giving my brother a chance means that on the other side of these three weeks I'll probably look back and wish I'd been smarter.

But on that other side is also Vancouver, a city halfway across the world. Regret feels about as far away. So does my dad.

And I *do* want to try taiyaki and kakigori.

"Sure, okay. I just need a few more minutes to finish putting my stuff away." I point to my backpack, and then gesture with my cell. "And to call."

As soon as Shoma leaves, I call home. I'm surprised when my grandpa picks up, instead of it being voice mail as he'd said it would be.

"Hello? Kaede?"

I'm even more surprised that he sounds wide awake. Has he been waiting up this whole time? I feel even worse now about forgetting. "Hi, Grandpa. Yeah, it's me. I'm here at Shoma's place. Um, sorry it's so late—you should go to bed now."

"Nothing to be sorry for. I just decided I wanted to hear

from you before sleeping." There's three seconds of silence—if he's listening to the news on the radio even now, it's too quiet for me to tell. "How was the flight?"

"Fine." Grandpa's used to one-word answers from me by now, so I don't know why I keep going. "They had some pretty good movies." I can't remember what I watched, though. My brain had been too busy worrying.

"Ten hours in the air—I hope you managed to fit in all you wanted to see."

"I did, yeah."

"Call again in a few days, just to keep me updated?" He laughs over the phone, the brief sound of it a gruff, rare thing. "And let's try for anything but the middle of the night."

"Sure. Good night."

"Kaede?"

"Yeah?"

"I really hope you enjoy this time away, to be spending it with your father and brother. Your mother would want you to. She'd be happy about this."

Something pinches in my chest. It's the mention of my mom and Shoma and Dad all at the same time, as rare a thing as my grandpa's laugh. It's being pulled in a bunch of different directions with no idea which one's safe.

"Okay, I will." I hope my voice isn't as wobbly over the phone as it is in my ears.

"Well, thanks for calling, Kaede. Good night."

After he hangs up, I flop down onto the futon, yawning as I open my backpack. I'm tugging out my clothes when my journal falls onto the bed. I wonder if I have time to squeeze in another entry before Shoma comes for me. My pages are looking awfully blank, and the idea of not doing a good enough job to pass makes me feel like throwing up.

The meaning of home. Home is . . . a mess of things. The dictionary says it's a place where we live permanently, especially with family. I don't know if I agree with that anymore.

I slide down until I'm lying flat on my back, testing the futon. It's thin but comfortable. Once I'm back home, it'll be my own bed that will feel wrong—too soft, too big. Our class had gone camping for a week for outdoor education last year, and it'd taken me forever to get used to sleeping on a bed again when I got back. I missed the bumpy rock ground beneath me, the stars blinking like lights in the sky, my sleeping bag a fat cocoon. All of it had been so new and strange at first, before none of it was.

I'm still thinking about how dictionaries aren't supposed to be wrong, about the guitar and the amp in the closet and how much they might be worth, about being careless in rediscovering this country with my brother, when I fall asleep.

13

I wake up hours later, in the dark.

I'm confused, panicked for nearly a whole minute, before remembering where I am. And my bedroom door's been left open a crack. The weak light above the stove in the kitchen shines in. Shoma left it on so I could see, probably.

I tiptoe into the front room.

The clock on the fridge says it's just past two in the morning. My brother's bedroom door is closed—no light peeks out from beneath it.

But I'm wide awake. And hungry—thoughts of the taiyaki and kakigori I missed make my stomach growl. And because I don't want to wake up Shoma by messing around in the kitchen, I decide to go out and find some food on my own. *Japan's safe, even at night*, Mom would say whenever there was news about something really bad happening to some kid somewhere in the world. *It's not perfect, and things still happen, but if you're not looking for trouble, it usually won't find you, either.*

I return to my bedroom and empty my backpack onto the bed. I slip my journal and a pen back into it and pile the rest into a wad I shove behind my pillow.

Slipping the straps of the backpack over my shoulders, I lock up the apartment with my key and go down the three flights of stairs. Outside the door at the back of Irusu, the five-yen coins still on the ground wink beneath the glow of the streetlamp. The lucky cat waves to me as I go by, as though wishing me a good journey.

I turn the corner and step directly into the beating heart of Shinjuku.

Lights are everywhere, all of them neon bright—yellow and red, orange and blue. The sides of buildings are lit up with signs and digital screens showing ads. Front windows of stores glow and wash out my skin as I move past them. People stream by on the sidewalk, nearly everyone in short sleeves because even night temperatures here are set to simmer. There is conversation and laughter and music from speakers strung up high. There are smells of cooking meat and cigarette smoke, hints of the beer Jory's dad likes to drink whenever he watches a hockey or football game on TV.

I walk past a pachinko parlor. The front door opens, and the noise of hundreds of slot machines roars out in a tidal wave. The karaoke bar on the corner offers ice cream and floats on their food menu; the one across the street lists honey toast and bottomless pop. Both of them are open twenty-four hours.

My stomach growls again, and I duck into a konbini. I buy late-night junk food—spaghetti-flavored chips, curry and rice that the clerk heats up for me—and a bottle of the same green tea Shoma had bought for us at the airport.

The clerk hands me my stuff and then holds out a

cardboard box. It's a draw box, with a hole in the top for my hand. "You get a chance at a prize with your purchase," she tells me, doing her best to sound enthusiastic at close to three in the morning.

"I don't . . . live here." I'm thinking about contests where the rules are you have to be a resident to win. "Is that okay?"

"You're not Japanese?" Her expression goes surprised. "You're a tourist?"

"No, I am—Japanese, I mean." That she assumes right away I live here makes me feel good, but also like I've just pulled a trick, was somehow being sneaky. "But I'm from Canada. I'm just visiting."

She shakes the box. "The prizes don't have to be mailed or anything, so it's fine. They're just in-store ones."

I pull out a voucher for a free iced coffee from the cooler.

"See?" The clerk smiles, looking as though she wants to ask me something—*Who taught you Japanese if you're from Canada? Why are you here alone? Where is your family?*—but then just says, "You can redeem it now, if you want, or the next time you're in the store."

"I'll save it, I guess." Coffee can't be good for jet lag. I tuck the voucher into my pocket. "Thanks."

I sit down at the counter that lines the front window and use a disposable oshibori to wipe my hands. The curry is hot, and I'm getting used to the mild bitterness of the tea. The chips actually do taste like spaghetti, but if I think about it too much the flavor seems more odd than good and gets hard to eat. When I'm done, I take out my journal, fishing around in my backpack for the pen. And with Shinjuku just outside the window as wide awake as I am, I start writing.

14

Dear Mom,

I know you only lived in Japan until you were ten. That was when Grandma and Grandpa decided all of you were moving to Canada.

But I hope that at least once you stayed up too late and snuck out and got to see Tokyo in the middle of the night. When it's not peaceful like dawn, but it's not rushed like late evening. There's this life in the air that seems almost secretive, as though it only comes up from underground once the sun goes down.

It's kind of amazing.

My brain's still trying to catch up to how I'm actually here. Home to all those things you used to tell me about— Pokémon and Miyazaki and *Shonen Jump*. You used to talk to me about growing up here, too, but not too much. It was so long ago, you said, and you were running out of stories, and things were fading from your memories.

I wish you were here again, seeing what I see. Then you could take back the word *fade* and use the right one instead— *vibrant*, or *real*.

You might never have wanted the two of us to move.

Even after you and Dad weren't together anymore, maybe we could have just moved elsewhere in Tokyo.

Because maybe then you'd be alive. Maybe there are no Mr. Ameses here. Maybe you'd be leading a whole different life right now, if you'd never returned to Japan for an internship after college. If you'd never met Dad during that time. If you'd never had me.

Shoma told me today that you were a great mom to him. How you loved him like he was your own kid. How it made him love you like you were his mom.

That would make you happy to hear, I bet. It made me happy, too. But I also felt this weird sadness, and this jealousy, and it was hard to breathe, as though someone were sitting on my chest.

See, I had to share you with him for three years, and you didn't even blink an eye at having a stepson. But I'm Dad's kid just as much as Shoma is, and Dad chose him.

I guess this is why Mr. Zaher looks at me with his worried eyes, the way he can't figure me out. Like I'm some kind of stuck gear, just spinning and going nowhere. Before school ended for the summer he used to call me into his office and ask how I was doing. I could tell my answers weren't the right ones when I told him I didn't want to ever forgive Mr. Ames, and how I hoped he developed a bad phobia about driving, standing next to his car every morning too scared to get in. Or how I didn't mind getting into trouble for fighting or not handing in homework. I always felt bad telling him, but it was the truth. I didn't want to lie. Lying to someone's face is a lot harder than just pretending to be okay (which is just a different kind of lie, anyway).

Also, Mom.

Dad's not even here in Tokyo.

You called it having wanderlust, the way he was, a thirst for the world so big it didn't leave room for the rest of us. But I don't know anymore. You reminded me about this old kite we had that we'd bought years ago in Chinatown, the way it would somehow always know to catch the wind perfectly and would then nearly break the line, wanting escape so badly. You said that kite had flight built right into it, down to every last inch of its frame and joints and wings.

Still, it hurts, hearing from Shoma how Dad didn't bother waiting around a bit longer to see me before leaving for Hokkaido, even though it's been nine years, so what's a few more days, right?

Is that why you left him? Before he could leave you first? Maybe you figured it out as soon as I was born that we were never meant to stay, that you were meant to bring us back to Canada. My name is the first clue, I think, what you loved so much there was no other real choice, you later told me. How "kaede" means *maple* in Japanese.

I'm sorry I reminded you of Dad sometimes. The way your face would close up even as your eyes turned unhappy when I said or did something that made you think of him. But you didn't use it as an excuse to not stick around. I think maybe it made you stick around *more*, just to prove you could, when Dad couldn't. It's why hearing Grandpa tell me how disappointed you would be about Jory still echoes so loudly in my brain. I imagine sometimes what you would say to me, and whatever anger would be there, it'd be nothing compared to how torn up you'd be over Jory. As though you could begin to give up on me, too.

Shoma's a writer, Mom. I don't know if you knew that, if Dad ever told you. But maybe you wouldn't be surprised, since you said he used to write for his school paper as a kid. (And he writes about music, about bands. Japanese ones, while you listened to all Western or UK stuff, but still. You guys would have had a lot to talk about, I bet.)

I wonder if him writing is his choice. If he needs it to help him deal with stuff or if it only happens to be the job that helps him pay the bills. I wonder how much he's like Dad when it comes to work being more important than family. Then I think about how he might answer, and I don't want to wonder anymore.

This journal is supposed to help me deal, even if Mr. Zaher never said it in those exact words. Defining home is my project, except the project is also me.

But just words on paper? Sentences that are code for what's going on in my brain, what makes my heart feel like it's being squeezed sometimes? What is supposed to help me find better ways of dealing with everything inside before it blows?

I don't know if I believe in kotodama.

It almost seems too simple, too easy.

Then again, dads loving their kids is supposed to be pretty simple, too. Just like big brothers being around for their little brothers, and not hurting your best friend on purpose.

Mom, I'm scared that I could write down every single possible meaning of the word *home* and still be confused. That I still won't be able to tell which ones are right and which ones are wrong. That I'll never remember what it feels like to have somewhere I'm supposed to be.

15

Dear Jory,

What happened was an accident, but it also wasn't.

I've been thinking about how fast reality can change on you. How reality, for one single second, can simply mean only thinking about doing something. Then how in the next single second, reality means you've already done it.

I haven't had the chance to talk to you about it yet because you won't see me. I've texted you, but no answer.

I don't blame you.

But I'm really scared, too, Jory.

What if this reality—the one where I made half your world go dark—is the one that's going to stick?

Have you talked to the doctors again? Have they given you anymore information? I hope your mom isn't still saying I've ruined your future when it comes to hockey, even though she might be right. I hope she hasn't convinced you we shouldn't be friends anymore, even though she might be right about that, too.

You know that old manga *Death Note*? Roan read it last year and wouldn't stop talking about it for weeks, he loved it so much, remember? So it's about a kid named Light who finds a notebook, and whosever name he wrote it in would die. It makes him all trippy with power, knowing what he could do with it, the ways he could improve the world by dooming someone. And even though cops try to stop him, Light honestly thinks he's just helping everyone out by getting rid of all the bad guys. He thinks he's a hero when maybe, really, he's only dangerous.

I'm no hero.

But your mom used to ask me to dinner nearly every night after my mom died.

Now she can barely even look at me.

I've become one of those guys Light tries to scrub clean of the earth.

She finally talked to my grandpa, who then told me what your doctors are saying.

How your left eye should regain most of its vision. How there shouldn't be any permanent, long-lasting damage.

But there's no way to tell for sure, since humans are just as fragile as they are strong, depending on what part gets hurt.

When we're on the ground looking up, a flock of birds can blot out the sun. But take it apart, and it's nothing more than a collection of breakable parts.

Tiny beaks.

Delicate ribs.

Wings forever grounded by one wrong move.

16

I take the long way around to get back to Shoma's.

It's nearly six, and the sun's starting to float up in the sky, but I get the feeling my brother's the sleeping-in type.

So before heading back, I do two things first.

I'm not really happy about either of them.

But I'm thinking about my dad and how he's all the way up in Sapporo. Just . . . there. Working, according to Shoma, but what if he's also hiding from me? I've got my box of questions, and I'm in this boat and chasing after my dad to ask them, but I'm being chased, too. And no matter how hard I might row, there's no escape.

Because deep down, those same questions are also meant for me. I need to reach my dad on whatever shore he's on so he can send me back out to find my landing space. *Dad, was it just me and that's why you walked away? Or was it just you, which means I was always okay?*

First, I make my way down to Kabukicho, following the directions on my cell. It's the area Shoma had pointed toward and told me it was too seedy to explore on my own. I hadn't drunk that coffee I'd won, but I might as well have, given how wide awake I feel, knowing I'm doing something wrong.

So what's so seedy about it? I'd asked him. The word made me think of drunk guys stumbling around on streets. Litter and bottles and weeds layered thick in the curb. Places in Vancouver where, driving through, my mom would tell me to lock the car doors from the inside. *Japan's safe*, I'd said to Shoma. *Mom used to say that all the time.*

She's right, for the most part. And Kabukicho's not exactly dangerous. It's just . . . not anything you'd be interested in seeing.

Like what?

Ah, you know. Bars, nightclubs, overpriced restaurants— places like that. Boring for a kid your age.

It *had* sounded kind of boring, hearing Shoma talk about it that way.

But sitting at the counter in the konbini, I'd looked up the area on my phone and realized why my brother didn't want to take me there. Kabukicho is Japan's biggest red-light district, meaning (according to Wiki) not just bars and restaurants, but places like love hotels and massage parlors. Mom probably wouldn't want me going there, either.

The thing is, there's something I remember about driving through seedy places in Vancouver, staring out the window at things I probably shouldn't have been staring at.

It's that seedy usually means resale shops.

That guitar in Shoma's closet looked like it wouldn't even be missed for a while, hidden behind his jackets and boxes the way it was.

And it looked worth something.

A large red archway tells me I've reached Kabukicho, but the area isn't electric or buzzing or even that busy. At dawn, everything seems wound down and exhausted. Store lights are dimmed, signs are flipped to Closed, and there are no hosts or hostesses on the sidewalks calling for guests. The air still hints of old cigarette smoke and food, there's trash kicking around, and a handful of people are making their way along the sidewalks, but whatever my mom or Shoma might have worried about me seeing isn't going to be seen. Not at dawn, anyway.

I wind my way through the few blocks that make up the district and mark down on my cell the locations of the first resale shops I see.

Just in case.

Suddenly there's a siren, close and shrill, and my heartbeat speeds up. It pounds deep in my ears and turns my mouth dry. Seconds later a fire truck comes down the street and zooms around the corner, and in my head it's spring again. My hands smell like smoke and fire, and I'm back on the other side of the ocean.

It'd been the week after the funeral. The house had gained a strange emptiness my grandpa couldn't begin to fill, a nervous silence the news on the radio couldn't touch. Going to school seemed pointless when I usually walked out of there not remembering anything and not minding that I didn't. Nothing tasted good, and everyone seemed afraid to look me in the eye.

Then one night, two in the morning, Grandpa asleep. I'd gotten the brick from the pile in the wheelbarrow in the backyard. Mom had paid me and Jory each twenty bucks to take apart an old raised flower bed that had stopped draining well. She'd rebuild it somewhere else in the back later, she'd said. When it got closer to summer. When she had the time.

I'd wrapped a dish towel around the brick, knotted the ends together, and soaked the whole thing with lighter fluid I found in our garage. I'd held it in one hand as I'd biked over to Mr. Ames's house, only fifteen minutes away. He'd been on his way home, too, when he'd been distracted by his vibrating cell phone and gone to answer it and hadn't noticed the traffic light had already changed back to red.

Mom hadn't felt a thing, they told me over and over.

But what if they were wrong, I kept on thinking. What if she'd felt *everything*? What if dying was nothing like drowning, or fire, or suffocating, but something not even imaginable?

My match had worked on the first strike, and I'd sailed the flaming brick through the Ameses' front picture window. It split apart the glass and made it all come raining back down to earth. The curtains inside lit up, became a skirt of flame, and then Mr. Ames was running into the room, stamping out the fire with his feet.

I saw his kids behind him, watching everything with wide eyes as they peeked out from behind their mom. They were really young, and I could tell how scared they were even from where I was still standing on the sidewalk. And suddenly I wanted to run. Not just because I could hear sirens approaching or because I knew I'd done something terrible and how Mr. Ames still couldn't change what he did, but because a small part inside of me wasn't very sorry at all. That small part of me was jealous of those kids for still having a mom and a dad. I felt it floating around inside my chest, the shape of it exactly like a small box full of sharp rocks.

Mr. Ames had refused to press charges. He explained to the police that he knew who I was and why I did it. It didn't make me feel better about any of it, though. His not being angry almost hurt, his easy forgiveness wanting something from me I wasn't ready to give.

I'd gone to bed at dawn, the light outside pink and purple. My fingers still felt slick with lighter fluid, no matter how much I washed. Behind my eyelids I kept seeing the faces of Mr. Ames's kids. The police talked quietly to Grandpa inside the kitchen.

My dreams had been bad that early morning—Mr. Ames hadn't been able to stamp out the fire, so it'd kept going, racing throughout the neighborhood, until it reached my house. I woke up with my heart going fast, the smell of bitter black coffee and smoke from burned toast in the air.

But now, here in Kabukicho, the only smoke I smell is the kind that comes from a cigarette, and the old man walking past me puffing away on it isn't my grandpa. The look he gives me isn't tired or exasperated, just kind of sleepy. And this dawn is one in Japan and not in Canada.

My pulse still fast, I turn in the direction of Shoma's apartment and start walking again, thinking about shores and landing places and how the ocean feels bigger than ever.

The sidewalks are already busier than they were, with people starting their workdays, most of them dressed in black-and-white business clothes. As I pass Shinjuku Station, instead of just going past it as I'm supposed to, I veer off and heard toward one of the Reserved Ticket kiosks right outside one of the gates.

Finding a resale shop had been the first thing I needed to do; finding out how much it would cost me to get to Sapporo is the second.

My fingers are even clumsier at the kiosk than they were last night, when I'd first arrived at my brother's place and was so scared I'd break something. I punch in all the information it asks of me—destination, point of departure, what day and time and for how many passengers. Whether I want window or aisle.

The total flashes on the screen and I'm calculating fast, as though going slow would leave even more room for me to start feeling guilty.

Forty-three thousand yen is how much it would cost to get from Tokyo to Sapporo.

I've got Grandpa's emergency cash card, worth two hundred dollars. That equals about twenty thousand yen. Along with what Shoma's put on my Suica, I have thirty thousand yen. Which means I still need another thirteen thousand yen to reach my dad. One hundred and thirty dollars.

I back away from the machine, thinking of my brother and his cool blue hair and open grin. Of liking him and wishing I didn't. My stomach clenches, morphed into a giant fist. Leaving the station, I find a 7-Eleven and test my emergency cash card by taking out a thousand yen at the ATM. The bill the machine spits out is practically brand new. Like it's not ready to be spent yet.

"Welcome," the clerk calls out as I move from the ATM and toward the store shelves.

I'm not even sure what I'm doing here, to be honest. The card works. I know that now. Even if there's a daily withdrawal max, I can take out some each day until I've drawn it all. On top of what I can get for Shoma's guitar and for turning in my Suica card, I should have enough. I shouldn't be spending much at all.

I buy a keychain from a little stand of cheap, last-minute souvenirs. It's a miniature stuffed mascot from an anime show for little kids, suitable for no one back home—not Grandpa, who I hadn't meant to buy a souvenir for anyway, and not Jory or Gemma, who I had.

The fist that's my stomach doesn't loosen the rest of the way back to Shoma's, despite carrying a blameless keychain instead of my grandpa's money. It's what I get for wanting things that cancel each other out, the way noon means it's not midnight, how noise swallows up silence. I've got questions I need to ask Dad, but I'm scared of the answers. I want to like being here, but I can't stay. I want Shoma to be a jerk, except I'm pretty sure he isn't.

The lucky cat beckons at me as I unlock the door at the back of Irusu.

I loop the plushy keychain around its shoulder and drop a five-yen coin at its feet. I want to make a wish, but I don't know where to start. My head is too full of my family and Jory and school.

In the end, I fumble out the stupidest wish before heading inside, stupid because of how much I actually want it to come true, no matter how much I might regret it:

That just for the day, me and Shoma will feel like brothers.

17

Shoma's still asleep, the apartment quiet and filled with low yellow sunlight.

Moving as silently as possible, I brush my teeth and grab a shower and change my clothes. Back in my bedroom I shove my clothes back into my backpack—there's not enough to bother hanging up. And when Dad comes (I don't let myself think about the 7-Eleven I was just at) I might as well be ready to go as soon as possible.

I call his cell, forgetting at first just how early it is. But it doesn't matter anyway since the call goes nowhere. There's just silence on the other end, not even voice mail. I remember what Shoma had said about there not being good reception up there in the mountains, and I disconnect.

Then I'm bored.

And because I don't feel like writing again in my journal yet, I decide to try to find something my *brother's* written.

I pull down some of the music magazines I'd noticed earlier and begin to flip through them, looking for Shoma's name in the bylines. When I see it over and over again as the pages blur by, I feel again that same mix of pride and sadness I felt reading that one interview of our dad's.

It's cool to know Shoma's interviewed real bands, that he's big and talented enough as a writer to be trusted to do a good job. Just as it's strange and hard to know how here on the other side of the world, my brother was happy and doing his thing, while me and Mom hadn't had a clue. Shoma's made himself a part of so many other people's lives, bands and their fans and everyone in between, while he made himself absent from ours.

The names of just some of the bands he's interviewed: sakanaction. [Alexandros]. RADWIMPS. tricot.

None of the names are familiar. They're all Japanese bands, and my brother's, while the only bands I know come from anywhere but here.

I pick up an issue of *Japan on Record* that has a special feature on up-and-coming bands from Osaka. It's ten whole pages of my brother's writing (*Text by Shoma Hirano*), complete with glossy photos of the bands to make everything look even more slick (*Photos by On the Fly*).

One of the bands is called Pine the Apple.

My brother got to do the interview with the guitarist.

This is the part I read more than once, half guessing at the hardest of the kanji:

SHOMA: *Osaka is like Tokyo's younger, rougher brother when it comes to music. Where do you think Pine the Apple's sound fits in?*
JUN: *We don't even want to fit in. We want to stand out, wherever we are.*
SHOMA: *Do you choose to write your songs in the Tsugaru dialect to stand out? Or because it's*

where you're from and your songs can sound like
home?

JUN: *Both, actually! Everyone carries their roots with*
them, what makes someone who they are. As a
band, our identity is in our songs.

SHOMA: *Are you hoping fans will hear that in your*
music? What home means for you guys?

JUN: *We write so they can find their own meaning of*
home in there. Their own identity.

I read other interviews and articles, steadily working my way
through a pile of magazines. I like Shoma's writing, because
somehow he makes even a stranger interesting. Kotodama.

But it also seems close to what my dad must feel for
photography. Which *does* almost make me want to stop
reading.

I wonder if Shoma walked into the airport yesterday as
a brother or as a reporter, seeing as we didn't know each
other. Maybe I was like one of his last-minute assignments,
the kind where he has to go in cold. Maybe he was nervous
to meet me, his little brother, when he's probably nothing but
excited to meet huge rock bands and famous musicians.

I wonder if talking to me so far has been easier or harder
than any of them.

I pull out another stack of magazines when some
binders—they had been leaning against them from
behind—topple over onto the shelf.

It takes me a few seconds to realize the binders are

actually photo albums, the pages made up of thin plastic pockets. The edges of the pockets are gold with age, from years of being untouched by anything but sunlight and dust.

The photos inside are of us. Our family. When all four of us were still together, living in our old apartment in Ikebukuro, back when I was a baby.

Mom and Dad could be college students, they look so young. They smile a lot, since they have no clue what is coming. And Shoma is a grinning teen. No blue hair or tattoos or earrings, and his face is rounder—closer to mine now than his—but it's him. He wears a school uniform in a lot of the photos, an uptight blue blazer and ironed trousers, and I find myself snickering at how proper he looks.

And then there's me, going from chubby infant to three-year-old kid. Most of the time I'm in photos with my mom, or with Shoma, or by myself. The ones with my father become fewer and fewer as I go from the oldest album to the newest. Photos of my dad, by the final pages, are few and far between—in his place is his growing restlessness, blooming like one of the weeds in the garden my mother was always fighting.

Part of me thinks I'm stupid to believe any of this can actually work out for the best. That somehow home will find a way to make sense again. Repeating Grade 7 would be tough, but I'd get through it eventually. I could just keep on living with my questions, always wondering why we hadn't been enough. How I was being greedy, maybe.

Mom always insisted we try not to hold Dad's nature against him. *You can't anchor down the wind, Kaede. Not everything is meant to grow roots, even those with someplace they promised to be. And sometimes that wind feels just as bad about it, not being able to help but go.*

I put the photo albums and music magazines back on the shelf. And I'm hungry again, even though it's only just past seven. It's been a few hours since my middle-of-the-night meal at the konbini.

I head to the kitchen and discover my brother doesn't cook.

There are no pots or pans, only a couple of chipped ceramic plates and some coffee mugs. The cutlery drawer is full of disposable chopsticks, all with sleeves or plastic wrap labeled with dozens of different restaurants. The fridge holds nothing but a half-empty package of kimchi, a still-sealed container of hamburg steak, and a single bottle of Kewpie mayo.

I wander over to the shelf full of CDs in the front room. It's tall enough that Shoma has used earthquake braces to hold it to the ceiling. The names of these bands are strange to me, too. The HIATUS. STRAIGHTENER. Nothing's Carved In Stone.

My fingers hesitate over this last band, their CDs in a long, neat row.

I know the saying behind their name, hear it all the time back home.

Why would a Japanese band choose it to represent what

they stand for? Did they choose it because they know some sayings really are universal? Because they want to make it big the same way, be everywhere with their music? Or is it just because they actually believe what it means?

I want to believe in that saying, but I also don't. It's a truth that is painful to accept.

Because if all things can be erased, it means both the good *and* the bad. If bad things can be left behind like they never happened and don't have to be forever, then the same goes for good things, too.

Sure, Jory might get better one day, my mistake fixed.

Mr. Ames will fade away for me, another mistake gone.

But home, family, friends—you can love them with everything you have, all those parts of your life that are supposed to be good, and it still doesn't mean you can make them stay.

All this time, on the other side of the world—maybe it's not too weird to imagine Shoma wondering these same things.

"Hey, you're up." My brother's stumbling from his bedroom, rubbing his eyes, dressed in yesterday's clothes. His grin is bleary and still more than half-asleep. I'd been right about him not being a morning person. "I'm starving. Let's go get breakfast."

18

It's as hot today as it was yesterday, and sweat drips down my neck as I stand there, staring at the temple's wall of fate. All those different drawers, with no way to tell what each held.

For a hundred yen, I can take my chances. Just drop in a single coin in exchange for a fortune that can either be awesome, terrible, or anything in between.

Tell me what I deserve, Goddess Kannon.

Shoma had told me the legend. How Sensoji Temple is Tokyo's oldest. How hundreds and hundreds of years ago, two brothers had fished a small golden statue from the Sumida River. Everyone believed it to be a symbol of Kannon, the Goddess of Mercy.

She's still inside this temple somewhere, hidden from eyes to keep her safe. But her worshippers keep visiting, constant unending waves of them. To pray for mercy.

Or for answers.

Over soufflé pancakes at Irusu that morning, I'd confessed to Shoma that my Summer Celebration Project was leaving me confused.

Why couldn't I have picked *any* theme but home?

Which was when he suggested we go to the temple.

Because Shoma had his own ideas of what the word meant.

"If you ask me," he'd said as we made our way toward the temple from the train station, "home isn't really an apartment, or house, or where your family lives. It *can* be, but I think it's more a collection of things like that. Like a well you fill up over time. Bits and pieces collected from all around you, the places you like best. Things you know down to their bones, people you can always find because you know they'll be there—those count, too. And all that stuff, taken together and piled up inside that well, is basically home."

I'd pictured a giant dark well, a box of tough questions floating around in it. I'd tried to guess where our dad was at that very moment. Likely on a cold, isolated mountain somewhere in Hokkaido, not a single soul around. Just the way he liked it.

I'd squinted up at the sun, blinking through the sweat that was already in my eyes. Overhead was the hugest red lantern I'd ever seen, which marked the entrance to Sensoji. According to my visitors' brochure—Shoma had grabbed one for me as we passed the info booth (*For your project*, he'd said)—the lantern is twelve meters tall and nearly as wide. I'd never seen anything like it, and, considering there were dozens of people lining up to take pictures with it, I wasn't the only one.

"So Shinjuku is home for you?" I'd asked Shoma.

"Sure." He grins. "My favorite restaurants are here. I like

how I get morning sun in my room. I know all the best routes to and from the station."

But Dad lives in Tokyo, too. In Nakano, just a few stations away. Doesn't he count as one more reason, being so close to you?

"And you, Kaede, are like that well. Needing parts to dump inside, to start filling it up. It's been so long since you lived here that it's almost like you never—" Shoma stopped, catching himself. Then he simply finished with "So now we're here."

I'd let it slide. I'd only said the obvious. "This is a temple."

"Temples can be a part of someone's home."

I frowned. "The way a favorite restaurant can be?"

He'd kind of laughed at that, and nodded. "Kind of, sure. This *is* a favorite temple for lots of people."

"But you meant something different, didn't you?"

"Nah, not really. But I think if you come here, you never really forget it. Wherever you go afterward, however many sites later, I bet you'll still be carrying a part of this place with you. And that's memory, and memory—well, there should always be room for memories in that well, too, don't you think?"

I'd nodded, still half caught on what he'd almost said, before he realized it might sound cruel when he doesn't mean it to be. How it's been so long since I've lived here, I might as well not have. I might as well not even be Japanese, I'm so new to everything. How I'm really, deep down, a foreigner.

The word is like a sore I keep poking at with my tongue, so it keeps hurting.

My blood's as Japanese as his, but to Shoma, it's not enough.

I've heard all the words for Asians born overseas and then raised there—banana, Twinkie, golden Oreo, nugget potato. Me and Gemma know all of them.

But even though I grew up in Canada, I was born here. And I look the part. So unless you hear me saying something odd or notice me doing something that doesn't fit, you'd never know I don't belong. You'd never know that sometimes I feel the same way in Canada, too. How just before coming here, that feeling of sticking out was for more reasons than ever.

I watch people line up for their fortunes at the wall of fate, to test their luck. They all seem so relaxed. As though nothing really serious hangs in the balance.

I wish it were the same way for me.

Shoma's over by the pagoda, cool in his sunglasses, quietly taking a work call on his cell.

I feel bad that he's here, having to watch me. But my calls to our dad are still ending up in that void of no response, which is centralized right over where he is, a cloud of non-Dad. Which means my family tree questions are in that same void, too, still needing answers.

(I'd asked Shoma some over breakfast, but he hadn't known much, either. "Sorry, Kaede. I guess I have a really bad memory, or he just never told me.")

A trio of miko crosses the garden behind him. Their skirts are fat billows of crimson, their white kimono tops as bright as fresh snow. Others work at the souvenir stand; one sweeps at pavement.

I'm not supposed to believe in things that aren't based on cold hard fact. The world's all about computers and technology now. Gods and goddesses and fortunes don't have logic at their core, but instead tradition and spirits and superstition.

Once when we were little, me and Jory had snuck into the neighborhood church to steal a bunch of cookies. It was a First Baptist one, the name always odd from my lips as I'd said it, unsure of its meaning. It'd been orientation for the brand-new Sunday school kids, which neither of us were in the least.

But that was the closest I've ever come to going to church, and cookies weren't enough to make me a believer. If you're not praying for the future, you're praying for the past. And the past can never be changed. Time never runs backward. Both are fact.

I knew that, even back then. I know it now.

Still, I find myself suddenly praying.

Because it's also a fact that people are more than fifty percent water. And water on earth never entirely disappears—it just hangs out in the air before coming back again as rain and rivers and lakes. If we can zap dead hearts back to life with electricity, or thaw flash-frozen people and have them be okay, why can't people just re-form when parts of them are still around, waiting to be picked up? Why couldn't my mom be the one to be collected and given back to me?

I know how childish my thoughts are. Babyish. Embarrassing. Which doesn't change where I am, how I'm speaking to an unseen goddess, searching for answers.

I go up to the payment slot and slip in my hundred-yen coin. I pick up the metal tin sitting on the counter, turn it upside down, and shake it until a wooden stick emerges from the hole on the top.

The number 112 is written along it.

My hands are sweaty as I carry it over to the wall of numbered boxes and find the matching one. I pull on the handle of box 112 and slide it open. Inside is a neat pile of small papers—omikuji—and I take the top one.

My fortune is written there in kanji, columns of black slashes and curves. For a second I don't know where to look first, all of a sudden no longer able to read Japanese.

Then, at the top, swimming into sharp focus:

Sue-kyou.

Bad luck to come.

A little kid runs by, laughing, an omikuji clutched in his hand. In my head the laughter turns into the sound of Jory's skull crashing against glass. The thud of the collision rolls up my arm again. I see spots of blood on the ice. My stomach swoops and dives.

I roll up the omikuji into a clumsy, messy strip and head over to one of the nearby trees. I find room on one of its branches and tie the fortune to it. All the trees have lots of other fortunes already tied to them, maybe even hundreds, all wanting to be forgotten. *Take away this bad luck, Kannon. Show me your mercy.*

Panic is a sharp lump in my throat. Maybe the goddess will skip right over me, I think frantically. Maybe she'll give me another chance before punishing me again. Mom's gone, and Jory's eye is broken, and I'll probably fail school—what else can possibly happen?

Then Shoma's back, the blue streaks in his hair nearly turquoise in the sun. His ripped jeans are gray today. His shirt is faded just so. Against the backdrop of the old-fashioned temple, his coolness doesn't fit. Anything he could be worried about has no meaning here.

He flicks at one of the branches covered with twists of discarded fortunes. Bad luck wobbles dangerously, threatening to become untied and land at my feet.

"So you got a bad one, huh?" My brother makes a sound of sympathy and then glances around, yawning again. I can tell he's ready to leave.

"Will tying it away really work?" I whisper. I wonder what happens to cursed omikuji that do fall to the ground. If a breeze comes by and blows them so far they can never be stopped. Does it mean bad luck without end, growing fatter over time like tumbleweeds that just keep going? To make someone forever sorry and still have it never be enough?

Suddenly Shoma shoves a five-yen coin into my hand. I

stare hard at it, at the little hole that's like a doorway in its center, my excuse to hide my face from his. My eyes are hot, and the edges of the world are all watery.

"Hey, let's go inside and do the whole tourist thing and pray. Might as well, seeing as we're already here, right?" Then he turns and heads toward the main hall without waiting for me. Like he can tell how close I am to crying and how I don't want him seeing me.

I let a few seconds pass before I follow. I'm careful to not stand too close to him as I flip my coin onto the platform and begin praying to a goddess who's just cursed me. So he can't ask what I'm wishing for.

I would have to lie.

Not about all parts of it. I wish for Jory to get better, to pass Grade 7, for my dad to hurry back to Tokyo so I can finally ask what had been missing from me that he'd left.

But I can't tell Shoma I'm wishing for him to stop being nice.

Because no matter how much I might have cried leaving my brother the first time, at least I don't remember it.

But this time, I will. I'll remember everything about it. Which means if Shoma ends up being just like Dad after all, him being a jerk and someone I'd be better off not liking would be for the best.

It would save everyone a lot of trouble in the long run.

19

Dear Nothing's Carved In Stone,

Why did you choose your band name?

That's the first thing I'd ask you guys, if I ever got the chance. Or get my brother to ask you, if he ever gets to interview you for one of his magazines. Because hearing someone else say it, maybe it'll convince me I still need to believe in that saying, if only so there's always hope.

How even if good things have to fade, then mistakes have to fade along with them, too.

How we might pay a price but then get something back.

How it's life.

I keep trying to imagine everything working out, all the bad stuff going away:

I stop missing my mom so much.

Jory sees again.

I learn how to forgive my dad for not being around.

I get to start junior high with my friends.

But, yeah, the truth is, even if all that happens, it still doesn't mean Shoma isn't going to forget about me as soon as my plane takes off. Other drivers will keep getting distracted from the road and more red lights will be run, so other people will still get killed. Dad takes being forgiven as encouragement to keep doing what he does, and we never see him again. Jory no longer wants to be friends. All the kids will keep on whispering about me.

So you guys see why I'm torn about that saying, right? How your name can mean great things but also sad things, and how not being sure is really hard?

His name is Shoma Hirano, by the way. My brother, I mean. He writes regularly for magazines here, magazines you guys have been in. The big-deal ones like *Japan on Record*, and *Discography*, and *Ririkku*.

If you don't know him yet, chances are good that you will one day. Not just because you're both in the music business, but also because he's awesome at what he does. He isn't going to be doing anything else, anywhere else, anytime soon. It's like his heart is so full of Japan, that his love for writing and for the music here is so great it's all part of his DNA, part of that well he calls home. And now he can't ever leave Japan without being badly damaged in some way, without becoming someone else. He doesn't doubt where he belongs. He knows it like he knows his own name.

Home.

I'm still figuring out what that means to me, now that Vancouver doesn't fit and neither does Japan.

It used to be so easy. Home was Mom and our house. It was Gemma and Jory and the local Mac's with their dozen slushie flavors. It was the wet West Coast and Hawaiian pizza and bike rides on rainy roads.

So what does it mean when I hear a train jingle on the

Yamanote Line and recognize it instantly? Or when the smell of incense washes over me, and I know I've been to that temple before? Or when Shoma says something really casual and offhand about being my brother, as though our family isn't as messed up as I know it to be?

What does it mean when the place you were born in feels both strange and not strange?

When it's almost eight thousand kilometers across the ocean yet still swims around in your heart, somehow close?

Mr. Zaher and Ms. Nanda and even Shoma think that writing in this journal will help me find answers, the right definition. How it's through words that I'll figure out which places and people and even things and feelings will make up home for me.

Right now, I'm backstage at a live house in Tokyo, waiting for Shoma to finish working. He's interviewing a band and then watching them play so he can write about the show. I can feel the music through my feet, in the walls of the venue.

As I'm waiting, I'm listening to yours.

This morning, after Shoma noticed me looking at your CDs, he imported a bunch of them onto my phone so I could listen.

At first, I hadn't wanted to listen to what *he* listens to. Because it seemed like him wanting me to listen was his way of trying, that he hoped I would try back. And him trying can only mean bad things for me, once I leave.

But of family, and for years, only Mom has ever given me presents.

So now I *do* kind of want to try.

I don't know how much. It's like a dare, and I'm still scared. But I'm here listening anyway. And maybe being stupid again, since I'm thinking of brothers, and family, and about how things can change.

(This would make Mr. Zaher happy, I know. Because it means I can be something other than sad. And it would make Mom happy, too, that I'm no longer running so fast from Shoma.)

I'm making my way through your albums, all the way from *Parallel Lives* to *Strangers in Heaven* (Shoma says your next one's called *Maze*, but it won't be out until next month), and trying to decide why you and Shoma remind me of each other.

It's your words, I think. The way all of you guys write and *why* you do—Shoma with his interviews, you and your songs.

My brother brings me into his space so I'm right there with him, so I want to stay and listen to people I don't know. You guys write lyrics, and I can feel them get stuck in my chest, like they're talking to me, right there by my heart. Both of you, with music and writing in your DNA—if you tried to shake it out, you'd feel wrong inside, as though something was set adrift when it was always supposed to stay.

Jory's like that with hockey. He's got it inside him, just that same way.

And what I did to him—I was the one who shook it loose.

I'd fix it, if I could. With wishes, through handfuls of five-yen coins left at a temple, dropped at the feet of a lucky cat.

But until that happens, it's one more reason why I'm scared to go back.

Why I don't deserve to ever know what home means.

20

I get to explore Tokyo on my own the next day.

Shoma has to be in Yokohama. He's doing a special feature for a local magazine, interviewing musicians from the area as they drop by *Analog*'s office. He's going to be busy until nearly dinner.

I'm tempted to go along with him. Japan's largest Chinatown is in Yokohama, and I want to see how it compares to the one in Vancouver. I wonder if seeing it would make me homesick. If I'd walk around just comparing everything, from the food to the souvenirs to how loud the vendors can yell about bargains. I want to ask Shoma to come with me, so I can point out those differences. It might help him picture what Vancouver's like, where I've spent the last nine years, the parts of me still a stranger to him.

But Shoma can't skip out early from work. And though I've decided to try the same as he's trying, maybe it's good we can't do this. After all, seeing Chinatown together sure isn't going to help me face going back, since keeping us more strangers than brothers is what I need most.

And I don't know if I want to be homesick.

And maybe comparing stuff right now like I'm deciding if one place is better than the other isn't such a great idea.

Also. There's someplace else in Tokyo I need to see even more than Chinatown in Yokohama.

"It's just Akihabara," I lie to Shoma as I slip on my sneakers and adjust my backpack, concentrating extra hard on getting the straps just right so my expression gives away nothing.

"What are you looking for in Akiba again?" Shoma's on his third iced coffee, and it's nearly ten in the morning, but he still looks sleepy. His blue hair is wild and pointing in all directions, telling everyone it's too early to be up.

"Souvenirs for friends." It's partially true. If I were actually going to Akihabara, I could, most likely, find something for them.

"You sure you don't want to come to Yokohama with me? I can't check out Chinatown, but it doesn't mean you can't go on your own."

My brother's worry makes me feel worse. I open the front door. "Chinatown can wait. And I only have to take the Sobu Line from here to get to Akiba—I won't even have to transfer."

"Hold up." He disappears into his bedroom and returns with his wallet. He pulls out a credit card. "Just in case. I know you have a cash card from your grandpa, but it's an international one and sometimes they don't work, depending on the ATM. So take this for now. And I'm texting you the address for *Analog*, too. Another just in case."

I take the credit card from him with hands that shake on

the inside. I taste something sour in the back of my throat. It goes by the name of Guilt. "I'll try not to use it."

"It's okay if you do. For things you think you really need. Like, food's good."

"Just no ten-course kaiseki meals."

Shoma grins. "Smart thinking."

I drop three five-yen coins—all that I have—at the feet of the lucky cat as I leave through the back door, trying to feel okay about lying. It isn't really that I don't want Shoma to know what I'm doing, but more that I just want to be alone for this.

It takes me just minutes to get to Shinjuku Station. The streets are already more than halfway to being familiar. I can guess where to turn before I even get there and almost always be right. I know which buildings to cut between to shave off seconds. Soon I'll be the same as Shoma, knowing shortcuts like I've always known them, dealing with the Tokyo heat as though it's nothing.

Instead of getting on a train on the Sobu line that would take me straight to Akiba, I get on a train on the Yamanote.

It's only four stops to Ikebukuro, so the ride's short. The station's not supposed to be as busy as Shinjuku, but I wouldn't have guessed. Low roofs, winding tunnels, rivers of people. I'm still thinking of beehives, buzzing and humming and alive. There are the regular station shops inside—cafés, bakeries, konbinis. A smallish bookstore, still large enough that I bet some of Dad's books are on a shelf inside, if I want to go look. But I don't, so I keep walking, and everything around me keeps moving, too.

It reminds me how it's easy to get lost in Tokyo. Not only where you are, but *who* you are. You can just walk into one of those human streams and follow along and stop thinking for a while, like a robot with no feelings. The thought unnerves me, makes me wish that I'd told Shoma after all. So if I disappear, there's still a chance of being found.

I buy a drink from a vending machine, take the Sunshine City exit, and start heading toward our old apartment.

I'd copied down the address when my grandpa had gone through my mom's things, trying to find my dad's cell number. The kanji had been faded but still readable. A place that once fit the four of us, where we'd lived together as a family.

The neighborhood changes as I follow the map on my cell. It's typical of most big cities, I think, this transformation from retail shops and restaurants and businesses to homes and driveways and parks.

But Ikebukuro still feels rougher to me, less slick than Tokyo—its name translates into *pond* and *sack* and makes you think of swamp-like things. The yakuza are headquartered here, I remember Gemma telling me with wide eyes when she'd been googling Japan. Jory had suggested in a hushed voice that if I ever went back to visit, he hoped I wouldn't go on my own.

I'll have to tell them it's safe. How the roughness makes

the place somehow feel more real than Tokyo, even. Like a crown stripped of its jewels and shine and glitz, made only more impressive for being bare, and vulnerable.

I peer up at the apartment building when I finally get there. It's just one of many on the block. Made of gray walls and half a dozen floors. There is laundry hanging over nearly every window. Satellite dishes peek out, silver faces turned to the sky. Bikes are tangled messes of steel poking out from between railings like rings on fingers. Across the street are a Family Mart and a coin Laundromat and vending machines selling smokes and ice cream and tea.

I read a story in the local paper once about a cat that fell asleep in a delivery truck. The truck ended up driving it all the way to the other side of town, far from the only neighborhood the cat had ever known. It returned a week later, safe and sound. Somehow it knew its way home, even though everything on the way back would have been different, would have been new and probably scary.

Maybe home always being a part of you is how a compass is built to always spin north. It's never forgetting how to ride a bike, or never forgetting the taste of something. One turn of the pedal and you're automatically balancing; one bite and you travel back in time.

Except if this is true, it must only be on the grandest scale of things. Like Japan as whole islands, the makeup of your blood, the network of pathways that form your brain.

Because I can't remember anything about this neighborhood.

But I hadn't expected that I would (or even that I wouldn't). Only that I'd wanted to see for myself where I spent the first three years of my life. Proof, I guess, that they'd happened here. How I once really lived in this country and had a dad who'd actually been around.

Standing here, feeling more lost than ever as I stand in front of this strange building on this strange street, the past stays a mystery. I thought it was smart, coming to see that I'd been real here once. But instead of finding some piece of the shore I need to land on, I'm continuing to just float around, no new answers for that box of tough questions I'm still trying to unload.

There's a wall of mailboxes just beside the entrance. There won't be a *Hirano*, but still I look.

All names of strangers.

The front door is the kind you need a key for. I press my nose to the window of the building. The lobby is small. Maroon elevator doors, gray concrete floors, silver-tone fixtures.

I have no memories of any of this, either.

The elevator opens, a lady leaves the building. For a handful of seconds, while the front door hangs open, I can choose to go inside. I can go up to the fourth floor and knock at the door of 44A and hope whoever answers might let a twelve-year-old kid with imperfect Japanese take a look around.

The door falls shut with a bang, and I move away from the window.

I'm heading back toward the station when I almost miss it.

A tiny residents-only playground tucked in between apartment buildings. It's practically hidden by a thick front hedge the shades of celery and emeralds. There's a small water fountain with rust in its bowl, a park bench, and one of those plastic horse-riding toys on a giant spring.

The memory comes fast, like lightning, so bright it leaves me blinking.

The feeling of being lifted by my armpits so I can reach the fountain to drink. The water had been lukewarm and had tasted of metal. There'd been no rust in the bowl back then, but a celery-green leaf had floated in, and it'd swirled in circles as I drank. An older boy's laughing voice overhead, telling me to grow taller. But to not worry, because he'll pick me up until I do, and he'd be careful never to drop me.

The past pounds behind my eyes as I keep walking, an ache that goes all the way down to my chest.

I thought I'd gotten used to the idea of Shoma deciding he didn't need a brother—him going quiet for nearly ten years was message enough. But it was a fuzzy kind of hurt, the rejection a cobwebbed corner of a room where light never reached in the first place. Now it's in-my-face reality, him being silent all this time after taking care of me as a little kid.

What had happened to make him stop caring? Did he see the same thing our dad did to make him turn away? The hurt is new and climbs all over. A thousand stings.

I see myself at the airport, three weeks from now. Watching Shoma walk away without a single look back, already on his cell to someone more important.

But then I remember Shoma's voice telling me how Shinjuku is home to him, without mentioning our dad. Who lives in Nakano, just minutes away by train. Who, it seems, has become a person my brother can also never find, a person who is also never there for him.

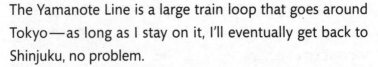

21

The Yamanote Line is a large train loop that goes around Tokyo—as long as I stay on it, I'll eventually get back to Shinjuku, no problem.

And it's a good route to take to just sit and watch the city go by. You can blank out or do all your thinking. Which means you can kill a lot of time, sitting on a train in Japan, if you wanted. Either going in circles or riding all the way to the edges of the country.

I don't know if I'm killing time. I don't know if I need to think some more about this summer trip or if I've been over-thinking it all along. I just know I'm more confused than ever about my family and nothing is going as planned.

Shoma's nicer than he's supposed to be, except he's only supposed to be passing through.

Dad's still missing, when he's the one I'm here to see.

My stomach bobs up and down with nerves. I imagine the lake inside that it feels like, its surface rippled by wind and fingers and sea plants grown too tall. My questions would be the fish lurking around, all snapping teeth and whipping tails.

Outside my window Tokyo spins. I stare at the stations as we go by and try to remember what I know about some of them.

Ueno, famous for its park with all the sakura in the spring.

Akiba and its electronics.

Tokyo, which sees more trains pass through each day than any other station in Japan.

Shibuya and its famous scramble crossing.

I've been on the train for more than two hours, and I'm halfway through my third loop around. We're coming up on Tokyo Station again when I decide to get off. I'm tired of being alone, which I am despite being surrounded by so many people. I want to find Shoma, so I can hear someone say my name. I think of how sidewalks seem to never empty, just as restaurants have plenty of tables-for-one. Japan is so full, but sometimes it seems to be a place built for the loner, how it's an island of the lonely.

I transfer to the Keihin-Tohoku line, wondering when Shoma's going to be done. The job's supposed to take him nearly all day. But he asked me to come meet him, and hopefully not just because he thought he had to. Since it's only half past four when I get off the train at Yokohama Station, I take the long way around to *Analog*'s office.

A few blocks into Chinatown and I don't think I have to worry about getting homesick.

On the surface, the Chinatown here seems pretty close to the one back in Vancouver. Both have huge arched gates marking the different entrances. There are tons of restaurants and souvenir stores, and the sidewalks are busy with shoppers. Things are red and gold and decorated with silk, with images of dragons and giant carp and good fortune.

But most of the shoppers are visitors, too excited over everything they see to be locals. Egg tarts aren't in every single bakery, and not enough shops are selling Styrofoam containers full of barbecued pork or fresh fish lying flat on slabs of ice.

But you can buy steamed buns with panda faces here, and I've never seen that before.

Baskets of dim sum are sold from sidewalk stands so you don't have to go inside a restaurant.

The streets, like so much of the rest of Tokyo, are swept clean.

I guess that's the biggest thing about this place. It's Chinatown, but it's also Japan—two maps side by side, so you see the shapes of both at once. With Vancouver's Chinatown, you can almost forget you're in Canada, if you let your eyes go unfocused and know where to look and where not to. There it's more like two maps on top of each other, so their outlines become one and the same.

It could be I'm just missing the point, though.

How maybe it's not about being okay by pretending you're somewhere else.

Because it's really about being okay despite where you are.

22

Analog's office ends up being in a pretty nice part of Yokohama.

It's a small building, but two whole floors are the magazine's, and the outside is all red brick and huge windows. It reminds me of the old warehouses in Vancouver's Yaletown area, how Mom told me they've been fixed up and so are worth a lot of money again.

I'm both surprised and not surprised that *Analog*'s way better than just some dive. I already know Shoma's legit, his work real and everywhere in Japan. But sometimes, talking to him, he seems younger than he is, like a kid playing adult. And I remember all over again that respected writer or not, he's also just my brother. With blue hair and tattoos. Who can't cook and likes sleeping above a café. Who's got an old guitar in his closet that he never plays.

I'm sitting on the curb just outside the entrance, getting hungry and thinking about all the restaurants in Chinatown, when he finally comes out of the building. He waves, smiling.

"Sorry, Kaede." He lifts a visitor's pass from around his neck and stops in front of me. "How long have you been waiting?"

"Just got here, actually," I say, getting up and brushing pavement dust off the seat of my shorts.

Here being *Analog's* office, anyway.

I'd wandered around Chinatown for a while, watching all the tourists shop and eat and wondering if my mom had compared it to the one in Vancouver, if she'd ever come to see it. I called my dad's cell again because I felt like I was supposed to be checking, and the same old silence had answered me. I followed a group of tourists as they made their way through the area, a couple of Bruins caps and Boston accents giving away where they were from.

I visited and learned about the temple that worshipped Mazu, the Chinese Goddess of the Sea, who protected fishermen on the open waters. I learned about the temple built to honor Chinese general Kwan Tai for his loyalty in war. I'd followed other visitors deeper inside and paid my respects.

My fingers still smell of the incense we'd been handed to burn.

And I'd pretended I, too, was thinking about sailors endangered by storms, about soldiers being brave in battle. When really I was just being selfish and praying for myself again.

Now me and Shoma are headed back toward Chinatown and its restaurants, both of us hungry. The sun's blistering, too hot for us to talk about anything that takes much energy.

"How was Akiba?" he asks.

"It was fun."

"Find any good souvenirs?"

"Not really. Hey, can we go eat?"

The thing is, it isn't just the heat that keeps my answers short. A section of my brain is still in Ikebukuro, in that old playground remembering Shoma being a brother. It made me wish I could be mean to him, to be the kind of brother who could just walk away, exactly as he had. But his eyes are somehow like my mom's again, telling me he cares.

I'm mostly distracted when I kick a series of rocks from the street into the mouth of a tipped-over recycling bin. I chant *Goal!* beneath my breath out of habit.

"You play soccer, too?"

I turn to see my brother watching me.

"Nope, only fooling around."

"I guess it doesn't compare to hockey."

"I guess not." I search for more rocks that need my attention, but there are none.

"Are you playing again in the fall?"

I slowly adjust the straps of my backpack. A part of me wants to tell him the truth about my suspension. To tell him whatever he wants to know about my life in Canada.

But hiding is what's smart—I won't have bits of myself needing to be collected at the end. The less of myself I leave behind, the easier I can forget about this trip.

"Yeah," I lie. "Preseason starts in September."

I hear Grandpa's voice over the phone all over again, trying to convince Coach it'd been an accident. Then the silence that takes over as he gets filled in on why it kind of wasn't one and that's why I'm being suspended. *The league is going to meet again to go over the situation, Kaede,* he says after hanging up. *They'll be hearing from your friend and his mom, and they'll want to hear from you, too. But for now, you can't plan on playing in the fall.*

Jory's mom—since then, she's looked at me like I've become a stranger. Or that somehow the universe has mixed me up with her son. How else to make sense of what happened? Jory lives and breathes hockey, while the person who takes it away from him is okay without it.

"That's good," Shoma says, sliding on his sunglasses. "I bet they tanked without you."

"Maybe, yeah." My sneakers scuff the ground as I keep walking. The truth is, I don't know how my team's done since I've been gone. I lost interest. I haven't bothered asking Gemma or Roan or even Perry to tell me.

My brother's too quiet, as though he can see right through everything I say, and my face gets hotter despite the sun staying the same.

"I didn't know you play guitar," I say, just to be saying something. It's the first thing that pops into my head, but it's also the *worst* thing, I realize soon enough. That guitar in the closet is supposed to stay forgotten.

Shoma laughs. "Oh, the one in your room. That's a bass guitar, actually. Like drums, but with strings. Rhythm."

"So how come you're not in a band?"

"I only mess around for fun—too lazy to practice enough to be much good. And too busy."

Too busy.

And he is. I've seen him, always writing or on the phone. And when he's not working and he's taking me somewhere, I know he could be doing anything else. Except that he has to say no.

"Sorry." The word comes out angry sounding, when I don't mean it to. Or maybe I do, just a bit. It's no one's fault but mine I'm here, but our dad being a no-show is just his. "You should have just told Dad you were too busy to watch me."

Shoma freezes for just a second, then keeps walking. "It's not about Dad. You're my little brother. I want to spend time with you while you're here."

"You can't fit nine years into three weeks." The sun is getting low, right in my eyes so they want to water. I wish I had sunglasses to hide behind, too. "The whole time me and Mom were in Vancouver, you were just . . . gone. It was Dad who bothered to keep in touch." At least in the beginning he did.

"'It was Dad who bothered.'" My brother exhales heavily. "Kaede, I was fifteen when you guys moved away—barely older than you are now. I was just your average kid who spent most of his time on himself; a baby half brother living on the other side of the world wasn't exactly a priority. Then I got older. I moved out and started working. And by then, you guys were strangers. I didn't know how to ask what happened along the way. Isn't that how you felt about me and Dad a lot of the time?"

I want to shout at him that they're just excuses, but I don't—because he's right. He'd never called, but Mom hadn't, either. She'd let my dad get in the way of asking her stepson how he was doing, how his classes were, if he'd joined new clubs.

And all my drawings, all my emails and letters—they'd all been for Dad.

"Was he home a lot when it was just the two of you?" I ask. There are more rocks on the road now, but I leave them alone.

"Not really." Shoma shrugs and pushes his blue hair back. "But I was still used to his traveling for work, from before you and your mom were around, after my mom died. He used to arrange for me to stay with friends, since it was only over-night, or for a weekend. Then it got to be half a week, then a whole one. An entire month once—Alaska, all that snow, all those moose and caribou. He missed my high school grad."

"That sucks." It really does. Some kids in Vancouver rent limos for grad; that's how big of a deal it can be.

"Well, that's Dad for you. And he's not going to change."

It's mostly gone now, my brother's loneliness, but I still feel the ghost of it around us as we turn a corner so Chinatown's just up ahead. It's an invisible bruise that spreads from him to me, reminding me how we're not so different when it comes to what hurts. And I'd always been so care-ful to keep our dad's absence wrapped up around just me and Mom—I never left room for anyone else. I never thought about whether or not Shoma was wondering where we'd gone, too.

"Mom would like how you're into music," I blurt out, wanting him to know now. That he had no idea, but he and Mom had still been kind of connected, even over a huge ocean and over years of time. "She was always listening to the radio at home."

"Yeah?" Shoma's smile is tentative, nothing like his normal one. "What did she like?"

"All kinds of stuff. English bands, though. I bet she would have liked your bands, if you'd been able to tell her about them."

"I would have liked to, for sure."

I keep scuffing my shoes along the pavement, uncertain of what else to say or of what comes next. On one side of the street there's bubble tea for sale, on the other Chinese folding fans.

"So can we start over?" Shoma asks this carefully, and I can tell he's worried I'm still upset. "You can pretend I'm a better big brother than I've been, and I'll pretend I didn't mind lugging you around for three years."

Don't worry, I won't drop you.

"I guess I was attached?" I ask.

"Yeah, because I was already this cool, even back then."

"I found some old photo albums in my room." My smile is real. "You weren't cool."

I can't see his eyes behind his sunglasses, but I can tell his smile, when it comes, is just as real as mine.

23

We decide on all-you-can-eat, and I'm already on seconds and stuffing more mapo tofu into my mouth when Shoma gets a call on his cell.

My first thought is that it's Dad. That my call just hours ago somehow got through in the end, and he wants to let us know he's on his way back to Tokyo. He's calling back to say he can't wait to reconnect with me. That he's looking forward to helping me with our family tree. That while I have other, harder questions for him, he won't run this time. How he'll answer everything I might want to know.

But it's someone from Shoma's work, and my brother's laughing as he agrees to something and starts making notes in a planner that he takes out from his bag.

"Hey, I forgot to tell you that we're going to Osaka for a couple of days," he says to me after he disconnects. "Sorry, I should have said something earlier. I'm not used to having to tell anyone about having to take off for work."

Osaka is hours away by bullet train.

"What happens if Dad comes back while we're gone?" Suddenly my tofu doesn't taste so good anymore. I'd just been about to return my brother's credit card, too, but now I stop. "If we're not here and he gets offered another job, he might just leave again."

Shoma picks up his chopsticks again, just as I put mine down. "I really don't think he'd do that."

"But you don't know for sure." My brother's eating calmly, which only makes me feel more on edge, nearly panicky. Without the family tree I'd been counting on to make up what I can't seem to write, my Summer Celebration Project isn't going to be good enough. The coming school year looms in front of me again, a huge shadow of dread. "I really need his help with my project, Shoma."

"I know you do, and I'm sorry I can't help in his place. Is there another part I can help you with? Maybe we can think of some more places you want to visit? Tell me what you have so far, and we can finish it together."

I shake my head. How can I show my brother how little I have? Letters to Mom, Dad, Jory, a band? A brochure from a temple? I don't want to see his face when he realizes he's been wasting his time with me. Talking about home with him, I think I say mostly the right things. But when it comes to writing them down, that's where I'm worried my words don't match what I'm feeling. "We need to keep calling him."

"It still wouldn't change the bad reception on his end. But if he comes back while we're in Osaka, I bet he'll call. He'll probably even grab the shinkansen and meet us out there. You never know. Stranger things have happened."

Shoma's voice—there's a bite to it. It catches me off guard, and I look more closely at my brother. He and my dad are supposed to be close. Both of them are artists, are the creative type, and Dad raised Shoma, too. It's always been easy for me to imagine them being a team, the same way me and Mom had been. Us against them.

"You almost sound like you're mad at him or something." I don't know why I'm defending my dad against Shoma. It confuses me. Shoma's the one who's actually here, letting me stay with him. "Dad can't help it if he can't call."

My brother pokes at his fried rice. He's back to looking younger than he is, as though he could still use a mom of his own. The lights of the restaurant flash off his earrings and his bright-blue hair. I count all the ways we still look alike—the shape of our faces, the shape of our hands. We have the same eyes and chin, too.

"I'm not mad at him, Kaede," he finally says. "I got tired of being mad at him."

"Do you *hate* him?" It's a new thought—that I'm not the only one who used to wish for a different dad.

"I don't hate him, either. He is who he is. Which is basically a lost cause. It's just . . . sometimes I'm reminded all over again how not all dads take off the way he does, and I get frustrated."

I guess I'm the one reminding him.

Shoma breaks an egg roll in two. His face gets this new determined look, like he's convincing himself as much as he is me that we're done talking about Dad.

"Anyway, we'll go to Osaka and have an awesome time. I won't have to work until the evening, so we'll have most of the day to kick around, eating okonomiyaki and going to places that'll help with your project."

I don't want to have an awesome time. I don't want to hear about going to a live and eating food in Osaka when I'm supposed to be right here in Tokyo. I have three weeks to figure out how to be okay living in a house without my mom. Three weeks to learn how to be okay knowing I hurt my best friend and how that hurt might be for good. The summer is almost over, escaping from me no matter how hard I wish for it to stay.

But this is what I do.

I smile at Shoma and tell him I think it'll be fun, too.

Because though he's only making it harder, the way he keeps trying his best to understand me, I've realized something:

If he stops trying, it will feel even worse.

24

Dear Jory,

Nearly everyone has blood ties, right?

Just like nearly everyone has ties to the idea of home, too. And to the idea of roots.

All those ties are supposed to work together, I think. But sometimes, for some people, they just don't. And instead they get caught between everything, not sure which way to turn.

That day on the rink, I think I was torn up like that, too. My head was full of anger, but my stomach hurt and was full only of missing my mom. Then when you said how I was just taking everything out on the team—it was like setting it all on fire, and I was suffocating beneath the smoke.

The morning had started out so normal. Your mom was at the door to pick me up for hockey camp five minutes early, like usual. You leaned forward from the back seat and honked the horn, and that was usual, too—not just the horn but the always racing to get back to the arena. You leave a part of yourself there, Jory, each time you have to go home. Like bees and their stingers—they also end up paying the cost for getting to fly around free.

I didn't want to go to practice that day, but I went anyway. Pretending to be into the game was the easiest way to get people to stop asking me how I was doing, you know?

I never told you how sometimes, skating out there, instead of seeing ice through my visor it was a paved road through a windshield. Sticks slammed at pucks with a bang, and I heard screeching tires. Coach yelled during drills, and it was sirens.

It became easy to shove a bit too hard during scrums. To get in a last cheap shot between whistles.

It was one of those cheap shots that led to all this.

Perry was still adjusting his helmet that I'd knocked off his head when he gave me a look that said I was lower than any dog crap on a shoe. *Kaede, dude, chill—this isn't the freaking Olympics.* He flipped me the finger as he skated away. He did it slow, too, so I couldn't miss it.

And that was when you said it, Jory. I was already angry for such a long time that it was like tossing a match onto a grass field gone bone dry, desperate with thirst. I remember your face, how it was more confused than anything, and told myself I was just reading it wrong.

So Perry's a jerk, but you're going to hear it from Coach if you don't quit it, Kaede.

Quit what?

Like you're looking to start a fight. You've been doing it ever since camp started.

It's called getting into the game, Jory.

No, it's called looking to start a fight. Your voice dropped here. Like you were already feeling bad about what you were going to say, but you still had to say it—because I needed to hear it, if only to help me. *Thing is, beating up any of us here isn't going to bring back your mom, Kaede. I'm sorry.*

And then you'd skated away, leaving your words to twist around in my brain, the same way your helmet was still hanging twisted from your hand.

Jory, this is what you said: No one on our team was the one who'd been driving Mr. Ames's car, or the one who'd been trying to reach him on his cell.

But this is what I heard: *You're* why your mom is dead, Kaede. I still have mine, though, and I don't have to live with a stranger of a grandpa, and you have only yourself to blame. Your mom is dead because she went out for something for you, was trying to make *you* happy.

Ten seconds was all it took for me to skate and catch up to you.

For my stomach to turn into some elaborate pretzel.

To ignore the Stop sticker on the back of your jersey, which the league now makes mandatory after too many head injuries.

I lifted my hand and smashed your face directly into the glass above the sideboards.

Ten seconds, Jory.

And reality went from awful to terrifying.

Mr. Zaher says this project is about my chosen theme of home and my last chance to not fail this year. But my mom being gone isn't the only reason why so much about Vancouver is hard now. That's how I know my writing stuff for this project also has to do with you, and how I need to figure out how I let that moment on the ice happen. It means I need to be so careful with my words. Like kotodama, using the right words for the right reasons. I don't want to be like Light in *Death Note* who forgets that. It's why he seems more like a monster than the hero he wants to be.

After Mom died, I started talking to God sometimes. Asking him to take it back, to tell me how to feel all right again. But you know how I've never been to church outside of stealing cookies. So how can I expect stuff from someone I don't even believe in?

I went with my brother to visit a temple in Tokyo this morning. It's not the God we know being worshipped there but Kannon, the Goddess of Mercy.

I've never heard of her before now. I didn't know her legend or why she's so special here in Japan.

But being there at the temple, she already felt less distant than God. As though she were actually real and right there beside everyone, listening to us pray for her to be kind.

I also told myself she felt that way because my praying for mercy meant I was praying for mercy for *you*.

25

Hi, Dad,

How's it going in Sapporo?

Shoma says you might not be online up there in the mountains. Which means you might not even get this email until you're already back in Tokyo.

But I'm thinking you'll be home soon, so no big deal.

I hope you're enjoying the location and how Sapporo and Hokkaido are much cooler than Tokyo in the summer. I wasn't ready for the heat here. Shoma says I'll eventually get used to it. He says that to me about a lot of Tokyo, actually.

I'm staying at his place in Shinjuku now. He's been showing me around the area, even though we have to work around his schedule. Tomorrow we're heading out to Osaka. We're taking the shinkansen pretty early in the morning. His job is really cool. It's like yours, since you're both in art. I bet you guys always have lots to talk about when it comes to work.

The food here is awesome. We have some good Japanese restaurants in Vancouver, but nothing like this. Things taste less complicated, as though being close to home means they don't have to keep trying so hard to be real.

If you come back to Tokyo for me while we're still away,

can you call? Maybe you can come out to Osaka to meet us, or I can leave early and come back with you and you can show me around Nakano. I also really need your help on my summer project for school. I don't think Shoma would mind too much, getting his time back.

Love,
Kaede

26

As the bullet train blasts us from Tokyo toward Osaka, the land changes, going from concrete gray to blue and green and white.

I stare out the window. I hadn't realized how little grass there is in Shinjuku, blinded by its huge cityness as soon as I arrived. It's around, but in pieces so small and scattered they're like leftovers, or secrets. But fields of it are now unrolling everywhere. Rivers rush into them and they poke up as mountains in the distance. The sky is a turquoise blanket over the world. Clouds dot it like cotton fluff.

More than Tokyo's tall buildings or city lights or population makeup, it's this bit of raw earth that suddenly strikes me as most like Vancouver. Most people think of snow when they think of Canada, and how it's so cold. But the West Coast only gets snow once in a while, since the ocean likes to change it to rain. And rain is what keeps the area so green.

I miss it, and I don't, and I long for Osaka to show itself through the window soon.

Even though it'll mean we're not where we're supposed to be.

I called my dad's cell again this morning, before me and Shoma left his place for Tokyo Station to grab the shinkansen. Nothing but that empty silence from his end, which now almost seems like a game. Hide-and-seek, or tag in the dark.

Still, when I packed for Osaka, I was careful to bring everything I own, just in case. My backpack sits at my feet now, smelling of guilt, heavy the way it is, too.

It's still possible, I think, Dad meeting us out there, if he gets back to Tokyo before we do. And then I'll be ready to leave with him instead of having to go back to Shoma's again to get my stuff. One less interaction, one less memory made.

And soon my three weeks will be up, and saying good-bye might be hard, but not as hard as it could have been. Shoma will get back to his life, and I'll be saved from knowing any more about a music-loving brother who will once more go quiet. Dad will disappear into some other mountain or forest or city, and maybe I'll hear from him again one day (but probably not).

There's another saying I've been thinking about, the one about blood being thicker than water.

It actually means the very opposite of what most people think it means.

Vincent had told me this as we'd TPed all the teachers' cars in the school parking lot. He'd made the discovery while researching for a school assignment.

So instead of it meaning that family is more important than friendship, it didn't start out that way. Originally, the blood they were talking about was what spilled during battles and wars, about soldiers dying for each other as they fought together. How by water they meant the kind that cushions a baby inside its mother, before it's born, every single one.

The saying, then, is really about choosing friends over family.

That what you get to choose on your own is more important and more valuable than what you are born with, no matter what.

Someone, somewhere, decided this was wrong, and that families, after they make mistakes, always deserve a second chance.

But I can't decide if that should include my brother and dad.

I also wonder if maybe the person who decided this just had really lousy friends.

Shoma's working on his laptop in the seat next to me, earbuds in. He's probably listening to the band he's watching tonight, getting ready with questions. I can't help but glance at his screen, curious if he writes with lots of notes or just by gut.

He pops out the earbuds. "Do you want to listen?"

"No, it's okay." Still curious. "Are they good live?"

"Well, it'll be their home crowd tonight, and these guys are young, new. Which means they'll either be amazing or fall flat. Pressure, you know? Home crowds are funny, the way they expect the best by demanding the most."

"Home games are like that for hockey."

"Yeah?"

I nod. "Because you know so many people in the crowd.

And they're all cheering for you. But sometimes it just makes you more nervous, and so you make more mistakes. Which only makes you even *more* nervous." The worst was being scared when all that cheering might turn into booing, when home just becomes something chasing you. We would skate out onto the ice, tough and cool, hoping we wouldn't let home down, not wanting it to turn on us.

My brother winces. "So you like away games more?"

"They're just different. Home crowds, they love you until you mess up. Away crowds hate you from the start."

Shoma laughs, and I do, too. "You know, you should write about home games for your project. I think it works."

I hadn't thought of that before, and I grin at him. "Maybe, yeah."

But instead of really smiling back, he's actually looking more closely at my backpack, the way I've tried to cover it up by pulling out my food tray over it.

I'd done my best to squish down everything this morning when I'd packed, to make the backpack as small as possible. And carrying it around, I'd been careful to keep it out of his way, so he wouldn't notice how it was way too full for a two-day trip.

But now it's all becoming puffy again, and even I can tell I've brought every single thing I own on this side of the ocean.

My brother's smile falls away completely, and my stomach falls away with it.

"What, you figured an earthquake might hit while we're

gone and there goes my place?" Shoma's look is very serious as he pushes my tray back into place and lifts up my backpack to test its weight. "Wow. You really did bring everything."

It's not even a question, because he knows what it means and why I did it.

"Nakano is super close to Shinjuku, Kaede," he says softly, setting my backpack back onto the floor of the train. "It would have been easy to come back for your things before you headed over to Dad's."

"It's easier *this* way."

"No, it's not."

There's an awful awkwardness around us that makes that first meeting in the airport seem a party in comparison. Because we know each other even more now, and knowing can make a hurt go from bad to unrecoverable.

"I was supposed to be with Dad this whole time, remember?" I remind him. "You're just babysitting. I'm doing you a favor by going back to Tokyo with him and letting you work in peace."

"Why do you think you being around is hard for me?" Shoma's confusion is complete, and I feel like I've kicked him. "I've never said that."

My gut churns. I pluck at a loose thread hanging from the hem of my T-shirt. "No, you haven't." *Can't you see the more I get to know you, the more I want a brother, even after I've left? And how if you get bored now, then I'll definitely never hear from you again later?*

"So?"

My gut churns more. "I don't know. I don't want you to get tired of me, I guess."

Shoma fidgets with his earbuds around his neck, as uncomfortable as I am. And his voice when he speaks again—it's gone funny, the way it did when he was talking about Mom. I've figured out this means he feels as bad as I do whenever my stomach starts to hurt.

"I know you're scared of being left out again, Kaede. I'm sorry that I sucked at keeping in touch with you. I should have tried harder." My brother sighs. "Especially later, when I got older and knew it and still didn't do anything. I *am* trying to make up for it now, even though I don't really know how. All I know are music and writing, and neither really helps me with this. So I'm still trying to figure us out, too. Same way you're still trying to figure out stuff for school, right?"

The back of the seat in front of me swims. Shoma is watching my face, and I can sense him freezing.

"I think what you do helps," I say. "I read your stuff and see how you're in there. I listen to what you listen to and hear what you like about it."

"I didn't say all that to make you sad." He feels bad still, I can tell, unsure of what to say or do next. There's an ocean of years between us, of people and things and *life*. But I also think that right now, we're more alike than we've ever been. "I said it so you know I'm not like Dad. Not even close."

"I know you're not like Dad."

"How?"

"It's simple." And it is. It's so simple that I'm mad at myself for always forgetting to look to see it. Even the way the world is racing by outside the window proves how true this is.

How when we love someone, most of the time, we can't help but want to go where they go.

The difference between Shoma and our dad is that Shoma's asked me to come along.

While our dad doesn't even turn around to notice he's already left us behind.

How do you know I'm not like Dad, Kaede?

"I know you're not like Dad," I say to my brother, "because you're actually here, while he's always been missing."

27

Hi, Mr. Zaher,

It's Kaede Hirano, from school. Grade 7.

Sorry for the email and for disturbing your summer. But I have a question about my Summer Celebration Project. I know it's for Ms. Nanda's class, but I think this is a question I need to ask you first.

Would it be okay if I don't want mine to be included in the display?

I think it'd be easier to work on it if I didn't have to worry about the whole school reading everything. I know home is an important topic, and it's why Ms. Nanda wants it shared. But now that I'm starting to write, parts of it feel important enough that I know it's only really meant for me. I hope that makes sense.

Please let me know.

Thanks,
Kaede

28

I read Shoma's write-up about who we're seeing tonight:

A band that still proudly calls Kobe home, punk-rock
Interpunct recently released their debut EP and
watched it climb the charts. Described as a cross
between ELLEGARDEN and Girl in the Sailor Dress,
Interpunct then caught the attention of live houses
throughout the Kansai area before playing a string
of sold-out shows.

Now they're back to play at Osaka Reverb, in
front of a very passionate home crowd.

Singer and lead guitarist Eriko Arai confesses
that while it's nice to go back home again, it's also
tough.

"I just think there's a special kind of mental
pressure that comes with playing at home, no matter
how successful someone becomes. Home is the one
thing that knows you from before things changed,
when you were just you. It reminds you of where you
come from, of all the things that came together to
shape who you are now. Like, I get it when someone
doesn't want to remember home, because maybe

their roots are too painful or uncomfortable to face. But I also think this is why it's so important to always remember. Home means nothing is permanent, good or bad. It means things can change. It reminds us, I think, that we're always still growing."

29

Shoma had written that Osaka is Tokyo's wilder, rougher younger brother.

I hadn't been sure what he'd meant by that, reading his interview in that magazine.

I get it now.

Two cities in the same country, bordered by the same waters and touched by the same winds.

But Tokyo feels like an elegant, refined cat, and Osaka a messy, bounding dog. They live in the same house but don't like to hang out together otherwise.

I tell Shoma this as we head out for dinner before he has to go work. *We have to eat okonomiyaki,* he had declared as we walked out of the hotel. *If you're in Osaka, that's what you eat.*

"Doesn't Vancouver have its Osaka?" he asks, laughing, after I tell him about my cat and dog comparison.

"I guess we make a lot of jokes about Toronto, which is out east, and they make fun of us, too. But I think most of it comes from just having separate hockey teams."

Shoma laughs again. "Ever been to Toronto?"

"No."

"Maybe it's awesome."

"Maybe." The pavement of the streets and sidewalks is still hot and beaten from the day, sunshine and summer and footsteps baked right into this part of the Namba district. My brother is cool in his sunglasses and blue hair. He looks at home here, just as much as he does back in Tokyo.

"Do you like one place more than the other?" I ask. "If you had to pick?"

"Between Tokyo or Osaka? Nah, I couldn't pick. Not for good. I mean, Shinjuku's home, but it doesn't mean I don't get tired of it once in a while. Some days Tokyo seems so wrapped up in itself, I want to hop on the first train out here and never return. And some days I'm here, feeling as though I've lost something, and more than anything I want to get back."

I try to picture Shoma not at his place, gone from his little corner of Shinjuku that's filled with all his stuff, everything that stands for who he is, and I can't do it. Imagining him out of Tokyo is making him a stranger. He'd be the brother with parts that don't fit, that don't really work all that well together.

I wonder if he thinks Vancouver means the same thing to me. How I could never leave there and fit in somewhere else.

I don't know if he'd be wrong.

I also don't know if maybe wanting him to be wrong is just stupid instead of being understandable.

Around us, Osaka swarms, its energy a built-up storm. But the good kind, the exciting summer kind, when the rain comes down in hard sheets and the air is full of thunder, and everyone on the block opens their front door to watch and smell and feel.

We reach Dotonbori, the area cut through by its own long canal. There are footbridges to cross the water, and all the buildings lining the canal are covered with lit-up billboards from floor to roof.

The biggest bridge is Ebisu Bridge, and we climb it until we're right beneath the famous Glico running man sign that marks where it ends. It's dusk out, so the lights around us are bright and blazing, hundreds of electric bonfires the size of your hand. Below the bridge, the canal's watery surface dances with color, all glimmering reds and yellows and purples.

I'd gotten a glimpse of Dotonbori from the hotel, after we first checked in. We're on the twelfth floor, so the view's good, even though it'd still been light out as I'd peered through the window. The city looks different during the day, the sun-faded half of a too-vibrant painting.

My brother says he stays at this hotel every time he's in town because it's near the live houses and venues and restaurants he likes most, without being too close to where most of the tourists stay.

I'm not sure that's the real reason, though. I'd looked up the rates and they're pretty steep. Shoma seems to buy whatever whenever, but I don't think most writers make that much. Which makes me think he booked it just for me, so I'll end up loving the parts of Osaka he loves, too.

Some of the ways the city is different from Tokyo are obvious, right there on the surface. Others are more hidden, like tree roots that only poke out of the ground with their knuckles. You trip over them before it occurs to you to look.

The kansai-ben dialect is spoken here, custom made by the area, with words we wouldn't hear in Tokyo. To my ear, the differences are slight, the way a language can be heard in different accents.

And escalators are flipped, so you stand on the right and walk on the left. I'd caught on even faster than Shoma had remembered, and his small nod when he'd noticed had made me feel oddly proud.

If you had reason to be invisible to the world, here you would hide your silence by joining in with all the noise. You'd talk your way along it, so no one could tell you weren't saying much at all. In Tokyo, the crowd would help you disappear by smothering you up, by just slipping into one and becoming one out of millions.

Dad hid from me and Mom after we moved to Canada. Maybe he's still hiding from himself, his work a disguise for how he's just not a family guy.

Mom, too, had hidden how much she resented him. The way she simply stopped talking about him just so *I* would, so she could escape having to ask me.

But maybe she created a monster, hiding how hard it was to be rejected, pretending we were both absolutely fine.

There's a coin on the top edge of the bridge, shiny beneath the lights as my hand comes to rest on it.

I want to think it was just left there by accident, that someone hadn't meant to toss it into the canal with a prayer and then somehow forgot, their wish left to drift, going nowhere.

And it's dark out. I can't tell how many other coins are at the bottom, or if there's any at all—the canal might not even be a place meant for wishes. The coin doesn't have a hole in the middle, either, since it's a one yen instead of a five.

Single-yen coins are made of aluminum, which means they're really light. They even float, if you place them on water carefully enough.

I nudge it over the bridge with a finger and hope it sinks. Vague thoughts run through my head as it disappears into the dark without a sound.

How I want everything fixed. How I wish my mom were also here visiting Shoma and Japan. How wishes of any kind aren't mine to make. How maybe the goddess Kannon is watching me right this minute, remembering I deserve that bad luck after all.

"Did you know Mom visited Osaka when she was little?" I say to Shoma. I'd forgotten until this morning, when I'd called Grandpa to tell him where we were going, and he'd brought it up.

"It was only once, for a couple of days, a long time ago,"

he'd said. "I think she'd been five or so, young enough to actually want takoyaki for breakfast." He laughed, but the sound was too full of memory to not be more sad than anything else. I pictured him holding my mom as a tiny kid, navigating Osaka's streets, the same way she would have once held me in our Vancouver neighborhood. It reminded me how I might have lost a mom, but Grandpa lost a daughter, so maybe in that one way we would always get each other. Just as me and Shoma would now stay connected, both of us without our moms.

"It stayed one of her favorite foods," my grandpa continued, "even after we moved and found out it didn't exist in Canada."

"You can buy it in Vancouver now, and in Richmond." I had to smile as I recalled my mom's exasperation after taking a single bite of the fried octopus dumplings, always exaggerated to make me laugh. *So shall we go, Kaede? Tell school you're flying to Japan with your mom because she's set on having real takoyaki?* "She said the vendors at Richmond's night market came the closest, but it still wasn't the same."

"It's not, I'm sure, though you have to give it to them for trying." Grandpa laughed again, and this time most of the sadness was gone. The news playing on Mom's radio was in the background, surprising me with how normal it'd begun to sound. How *not* strange. Mom would say it's a good sign, I know, this adjustment. "Have fun in Osaka, Kaede, and I'll see you soon."

"I think I might have known once that she visited," Shoma says, "but it's been a while. Still, it doesn't surprise me, her having come here. Osaka's great."

It's not supposed to be easy talking about my mom with my brother. Except it's become that way, and from Shoma's smile, I can tell it's easier for him, too.

"It's weird, thinking she might have once stood in this very same spot, seeing what we're seeing," I say. *Did you ever make wishes from here, Mom? If so, what might you have wished for?* "Though I don't know if she ever came to this part of the city."

"I bet she did. It's like eating takoyaki when you come— if you're visiting Osaka, you're going to visit Dotonbori. You'll want to see the Glico ad, all the signs everywhere, the canal." Shoma leans his elbows on the bridge and peers down into the water.

I glance at the ad over his shoulder. It's huge, over twenty meters tall, and all lit up. "If there's a photo of her in front of that, I haven't seen it."

"Maybe your grandpa knows. Maybe he was even the photographer. You can ask when you get back."

I could. I might. It's weird to think of Grandpa outside of Canada, too.

"I wonder how hard it was for her to leave Japan." I run my finger along a crevice in the stone of the bridge, keep my eyes averted from Shoma's. "When she was a kid, I mean. Not the second time, when she left with me."

"Well, she would have been around your age. So imagine leaving Vancouver now for some whole other country. Home, suddenly halfway across the world."

It wouldn't be the same, though. Mom had left with her folks. They'd left and made a home as a family. I'd be leaving with Grandpa, who's family mostly because it says so on the form my mom had filled in ages ago.

I run my finger back the other way along the crevice. Home. The more I think about that word, the larger it keeps growing—more important, more vital. How can I hold on to all of it?

What if my coming here means the world is being realigned? Being reset so some new fate is now waiting in store for me? So it turns out that Japan is where I'm supposed to be instead of with Grandpa back in Vancouver? There's a strong and stubborn pull from this place, making me feel like I've been here for years. Like I never left.

I glance up at my brother. "You think Mom would have found it easier leaving the second time, then?"

Shoma nods. "Yeah, I do. She wouldn't have been a kid anymore."

"I don't know if her being older mattered all that much." Mom would have been around the same age Shoma is now, but already a mom to two kids. I try again to picture him packing up his life here for somewhere else in the world, and it's still impossible. He walks around all confident, making me doubt he's ever unsure of himself. But take away everything he loves and knows, and I can wonder.

"Sure it would have," he says. "And she and Dad had just

split. Your mom was probably *happy* to leave. She had nothing to keep her here."

I stare at my brother, see him as an awkward teenager in his old school uniform, and my heart squeezes. Suddenly I'm sad, and sorry, and there's an expression on his face that says he's feeling the same way. I wish my mom had let herself talk more about Shoma when she'd had the chance. That she would have let herself keep loving him, to dare to love him more.

"She never said," I start, trying to pick just the right words, "but I think leaving the second time was just as hard."

"Because she was a single mom?"

"Because she couldn't bring you with her."

My brother's eyes change as his grin curls, telling me I was right about him being sad a second ago. "Like I said— cool even back then."

I grin back, liking having a joke that's just ours. "You weren't cool at all—like I said."

Before we leave, Shoma makes me stand in front of the Glico ad with him for a selfie on his cell. We throw up peace signs with our fingers, our grins ending up so wide they're nearly the biggest things in the photo. He makes me take one with my cell, too. *I think it takes real talent to take such awful selfies, Kaede.* He swears to me that he sees lots more coins in the canal, all winking up at him, telling us to wish away. Neither of us have five-yen coins, so we send bronze and silver of all sizes through the air. They land in the water with splashes. We name each of them, the silly wishes they stand for—An Awesome Dinner, Band Don't Blow It Tonight, Cooler Weather.

When our pockets are empty of coins, we start walking again, weaving our way along the sidewalks. The lights of Dotonbori reflect off the canal in slow, colored ripples. We're not lost, but if we were, they could be flashlights in the dark, helping guide us home.

30

Dear Dad,

You and Shoma are both artists, but I think he's thought a lot more about you being a photographer than you have about him being a writer.

When he was growing up and you were gone somewhere for a job, your absence was still at home with him. It reminded him of your work and why you weren't there being a dad. It was like that until he got old enough to move out. And even if he was okay with everything by then, he was probably still glad not to be living with a ghost anymore.

Now that I'm here in Japan, I know I'm dragging the past back up for him. For me, too.

But not for you, and that feels kind of unfair. You're still in Hokkaido, far away from where you promised to be, avoiding cell phone reception and the dull reality of us.

Dad, sometimes I really do wonder—do you know what day it is, even? The month or the year?

How deep do you need to go to escape?

We have scales to measure things that don't really matter. Everyday things like packages we need to mail, or how much weight we've lost overnight, or how much flour or milk to use when making breakfast.

What about the things we can't hold in our hands but that are about a hundred times more important? What about all those things we can't touch that feel like they mean everything?

If you think about how much space me and Shoma take up in your brain, how much energy you use up thinking about us, I bet it's nothing compared to how much we give you in ours, how much energy we use up. It's a grain of sand to a whole beach, a single flash of light to the sun's million megawatts.

Sand that's really deep can be dangerous.

We can burn our eyeballs if we stare directly at the sun.

Sometimes I think it's you who loses out. The way you decided to stop seeing us, even though we were always right there.

And then I change my mind, and it's me and Shoma who end up being the losers.

Because here's Shoma, trying to make up for you. He's my brother, but sometimes he remembers you're missing and tries to act like a dad.

And here's me, calling you again to check if you care. It's become a bad habit now, always checking. It reminds me of scars, actually, this bad habit I've picked up. My friend Donovan got chicken pox when he was ten. His mom told him to not pick off the scabs or he'd get scars. But he couldn't stop checking them to see if they were healing, and now he's got scars all over. He doesn't care that he has them, but he doesn't deny they're there.

I'm backstage at this live house in Osaka, waiting for Shoma. Music comes through the walls. I could be listening to more music on my cell. Or I could just be online on my cell, surfing and looking at nothing important.

Instead, like Donovan, I'm checking for signs of *healing*.

Dad, the smell of flowers is everywhere. There are bouquets in the room, sent from friends of the band to celebrate their show tonight. When I saw all those flowers, the first thing I thought of was Mom's funeral. That day was such a huge and awful explosion of sadness and painfully bright colors. I remember that you and Shoma had sent a bouquet of sunflowers, the kind she'd loved the most. Except I knew, even then, that Shoma had been the one to order them.

I'm not as mad at you as I used to be. I'm working you out of my system, I guess. Or working around you. You're the blind spot I have to be careful about when I'm riding my bike.

The thing is this—if your needing to always be away is anything like how Shoma needs music and writing, or the way Jory needs hockey, then I think I'm beginning to understand, to be able to see things from your point of view.

And if you'd been here tonight watching this show, you'd get why that is.

Because you wouldn't have missed the expression on

everyone's faces—Shoma's, the people in the crowd, the people on stage. They looked like they were home. Like they couldn't imagine being anywhere else in the world.

The way, I think, you never looked when you were home with us.

31

Dear Nothing's Carved In Stone,

Would you guys agree with me that being onstage—being in a band—can be home? The same way writing and playing hockey and the act of escape can also be home?

Standing up there, I bet you feel almost powerful, and therefore safe.

But fans—I see their faces and how they want a part of you.

Which means you must also feel vulnerable, being home or not.

I'd ask if this is why *Silver Sun* has songs that go from light to dark. From "Spirit Inspiration" to "PUPA" to "Inside Out," with their lyrics about being born again, to creating change, to maybe being trapped.

Jory's eye, the way it chases me like I'm the one thing it can see—how I hurt him reminds me just how dark home can suddenly be. How I'm scared to go back because that part of the world's gone dark for me, too. And I always imagined Shoma as being lucky, not having a dad who ran. But seeing him now, I know getting to stay here instead of moving away like I did doesn't mean things were easier for him.

A part of me doesn't want to admit it might be possible.

How anyone can be damaged, home or not. That no matter how secure you feel on that stage, however much you love your band, you might still need saving of some kind.

You guys give me hope about Jory, by the way. How one day we can be friends again, despite it all.

Because friends and friendships, the sometimes unmaking of those friendships—Nothing's Carved In Stone wouldn't even exist if not for one unmaking in particular. And that unmaking itself might one day come back together still.

Shoma told me all about ELLEGARDEN. How they were this huge band who broke the hearts of all their fans seven years ago when they decided to take a break. So each member went off and started their own band. Shinichi was their lead guitarist, and he met up with Hinatch, who would play bass for Nothing's Carved In Stone. Then they found Oniy, who would play drums. Then they asked Taku to join, to be their singer and to play rhythm guitar. And that's who you guys are now, how you built the home that is your band and friendship.

But roots never really die.

You can turn your back on them, but you still wear them as invisible scars, since you wouldn't exist the same way without them. We're only standing above ground because of how sturdy our roots are.

There's a photo online of you guys from Rising Sun Rock Festival, two years ago. In it, you're all goofing around with two other guys.

One of them is Takeshi, who used to sing for ELLEGARDEN. And just as Shinichi went and started Nothing's Carved In Stone, Takeshi went off and started the HIATUS.

That photo of the two of them together tells me how they're still friends, still connected through their roots. It tells me that the unmaking of friendships doesn't have to be permanent. They might never be the same again, but you can remake them in different ways.

Me and Jory can still be fixed, even if we don't ever play hockey together again.

We'll be an ocean apart, but what if me and Shoma can somehow still be brothers?

After Mom died, life filled up with cracks, all the new ways I felt lost. My house felt strange. Family was strange. I kept falling in those cracks. So I flew halfway around the world to learn how to not be lost anymore, to remember how home felt. And Shoma—he's telling me home can be anywhere, as long as it matters.

You guys actually played at the live house I was at tonight. Years ago, when you were just starting out. There's a wall of photos backstage of all the bands that ever played there, and I found yours. "Nothing's Carved In Stone, Parallel Lives Tour, 2009. Thank you, Osaka Reverb! Photo by SOUND SHOOTER." Signed by you guys and everything, four grins as huge as the world.

It was cool to see that photo and know you guys would stick, even if *you* hadn't known that at the time. Just like it was cool to know that whatever you ended up going through, you'd still keep making music. You'd still be around, writing songs, making the world spin, and asking for fans to follow.

In two days, it's Rock in Japan, which Shoma says is the biggest outdoor music festival in Japan. It's a big deal for him, getting to write up one of its stages. He's really excited about who he gets to see play, who he gets to meet.

I hope you guys play "November 15th." It's a song about finding your way. Which means it's also a song about home.

It's one of Shoma's favorites.

And one of mine, too.

32

Shoma glances into the window of the store we're passing by.

"Hey, it's a Frets," he says, stopping on the sidewalk to look at the display of guitars. "I forgot there's a location here in Osaka. Let's check it out."

"But—"

"C'mon, it'll be quick."

We're in a semi-rush, walking fast to the train station to make our shinkansen back to Tokyo. Shoma had slept in—and because of what I almost did last night, I let him. I was sure he'd see my guilt as soon as he woke up, reason enough to want to hide for as long as possible.

But he hadn't noticed. I almost wish he had, just so he would learn to be more careful around me, so he would stop bothering to be nice.

He'd left his wallet on the desk in the hotel while he'd grabbed a shower. He assumed it would be safe with me, never thinking about someone he trusts stealing from him.

But he's never really had a brother. Especially not a brother terrified of the coming autumn, helpless in the face of sure doom. A squirrel on a highway feels the vibrations of a nearing speeding semi and freezes. A bird flies into a window and is stunned breathless. All those people who made the mistake of watching that videotape in *The Ring*.

I'd checked inside the wallet. Full of cash. Along with his credit card I still hadn't returned, it was more than enough for a plane ticket to Sapporo.

How many ways can you betray family and still have them forgive you? I'd wondered, taking out the cash to hold it, my heart pounding. What if you convince yourself that their betraying you first makes it okay? What kind of betrayals just can't be fixed in the end?

Because skipping out on Shoma to go and find Dad definitely qualified as a betrayal. Telling myself I would be doing my brother a favor was one thing; still going after he told me he thought Dad was a lost cause and how I should give up on him was another.

And there was something else now, another reason why I wanted to find my dad, and it wasn't just about needing his help with my project, or even to finally answer all the questions I've been carrying around in that box in my head.

Instead it was a reason so crazy I was still only circling it, not yet ready to admit its existence, especially not to the person telling me I was wasting my time, searching for the unsearchable. Shoma, left behind when *he'd* been a kid.

The reason was this:

I was starting to hope that once I met our dad, he'd ask me to stay in Japan with him. As his kid again, and this time for good.

Then I'd heard Shoma turn off the shower, and I'd shoved

the money back into his wallet so fast I nearly sent all of it flying to the floor. I was actually relieved to not have to think about it anymore. Just as I was relieved when I called Dad's cell again after Shoma was asleep and there was still no answer. And in the morning, I dreaded Shoma picking up his wallet, sure he'd notice I'd been digging around.

I'd hit snooze when his alarm went off, delaying.

In Frets now, I know if we miss our train, it's more my fault than his.

Inside, guitars are fire-engine red to cloud white to deep gold. They hang from racks on the wall—electric, acoustic, bass. The ceiling lights glint off their curves and strings. There are testing stations set up on the far side of the room. Customers hang around, browsing.

Shoma disappears down one of the aisles, exploring.

I stare up at walls of guitars and think about secrets.

We did a unit on the ocean for science last spring, where we learned that conch shells found washed up on the beach are really just outer skeletons made of calcium carbonate.

But when their soft parts had been around, they might have once made a pearl.

You can hear the ocean in an empty shell, a soft and constant roar.

If you blow into the end of one, the sound it makes will remind you of trumpets.

Just bones. Just calcium. But so much more.

Guitars are wells of secrets to me, too, even if I can break them down to things I know—wood and metal, steel and strings. Add in fingers and determination and somehow there's music.

There's a girl at one of the testing stations. She's got her amp blasting; I can hear her play. Her fingers move fast between chords, and carefully. I remember how my own hands had felt so heavy and uncoordinated as I'd lit a fire and threw a brick. As she plays, her expression is the same as those onstage, as Shoma's as he watches a show, as those of the crowd all around him.

It says *home*.

The girl looks up from beneath a thick fringe of purple hair. "Sorry, I didn't know anyone was waiting."

I shove my hands into my pockets. Guitars are breakable, just like glass windows. Just like eyesight. "Only watching. And listening."

She glances at my hands in their pockets. "You don't play?"

"I'm waiting for my brother. He plays bass."

"Well, since you're waiting—here. Try." And before I can say anything, she's getting up and holding the guitar toward me.

It's painted a soft deep black. The neck is skinny, its strings fragile. I don't move.

"Here, I'll take it." Shoma comes up from behind me, and the girl passes it to him before leaving. "Thanks. C'mon, Kaede, we still have a few minutes."

I watch him, feeling stupid as he sits down on the bench. He grabs a silver pick from a bucket at his feet. "You don't play guitar, even," I mutter. "And we're going to miss our train."

"Will you just relax and get over here?"

I sit down beside him. I keep my hands stuffed in my pockets.

Maybe it's just the sound of the guitar that does it, or that it's my brother who's playing, but a wave of loneliness hits when he starts playing. It tells me everything's gone wrong, even if I want to believe otherwise.

It was supposed to be easy, leaving this time around.

I'd built up nearly ten years' worth of ready and thought it would be enough.

I still haven't found Dad. My Summer Celebration Project is nothing close to being an excellent effort. My family tree is mostly blank, this side of the ocean still the unknown.

My box of tough questions? Still lodged in my head, taking up space it doesn't deserve.

And in two weeks, Shoma's taking me to the airport. He'll say, *See you later*, except we both know he won't. He'll go on writing about music, connecting to bands and readers more than he'll connect with me.

"I started with guitar, you know," he says, suddenly stopping playing. "When I was just a bit older than you. Band, for school."

"Why'd you switch to bass?" Shoma always seems so sure of what he's chosen to do. It's hard to imagine him once having to work things out, even as a kid. But then I think about him saying how he's now working on figuring *us* out. And I think about how he's ended up fine.

"I discovered this band called STRAIGHTENER," Shoma says. "Still awesome, by the way, and still one my favorites. Anyway, their bassist blew me away."

I have to grin because I know who he's talking about. "Hinatch is Nothing's Carved In Stone's bassist, too."

"Sure is."

"How did you know to switch to bass?" I think of what he'd said about home being a collection of important things. "To find that part of home for you?"

"Well, bass sometimes gets overlooked. But when it's good, you never forget hearing it, and Hinatch had made himself great. He made playing bass part of this home that could never be torn down or taken away. He made it his own."

Shoma, having to live with a ghost for a dad—that home had been too shaky for him to stay.

He glances over at me. "Are you worried about hockey not working out?"

I'm pretty sure he's already put together how I'm suspended. And I can keep lying about it, but I decide not to. This summer started out strange, and horrible, but . . . it's not so much anymore. And it might be stupid of me, but I don't want that to change back.

"I'm suspended from the league," I say slowly. "So I probably won't be playing in the fall."

"Right, got it. That sucks, and I'm sorry." Shoma strums out more notes and says nothing else.

"I'm not even sure I want to keep playing." Admitting it is easier than I thought it would be. It actually feels good to say it out loud. "But Jory loves it, and it seems like I should, too."

"But you're not Jory." He hands me the guitar and the pick. "You're also not me."

I adjust the shoulder strap, my fingers clumsy and cold. The silver plastic triangle feels flimsy in my grip. And suddenly I'm scared. Not about Shoma laughing at how bad I'll sound, but because I care he's going to see how we have nothing in common.

"So, first thing—you need to stop holding everything like it's made of glass." Shoma gives me a grin that says he understands, and I take a deep breath. "You're new, Kaede, not destructive."

Destructive.

I see flashes of broken glass—sprinkled on a hedge in front of a house, lying on the ice of a skating rink. The strings blur and waver as I look down at them. But then Shoma's adjusting my posture, telling me to watch my elbows and relax my shoulders. I curl my left hand around the neck of the guitar and press down on the frets with my fingertips. I hold the pick in my right hand, between my thumb and first finger so the pick's top point sticks out like a shark fin from the water.

Sharks—they can swim just fine. Water is their home.

They don't worry about getting hurt or drowning. They know they can, but it doesn't stop them from feeling powerful.

"And then you just"—Shoma mimics the motion with his arm as he speaks—"bring the pick down along the strings."

So I do.

33

Dear Jory,

I'm on the shinkansen, headed back to Tokyo from Osaka. The train moves so smoothly, you can barely tell anything is happening unless you look out the window. It's like being on a breakaway and there's nothing but wide-open ice in front of you, and you can just keep going.

Shoma's sitting beside me, his laptop on the pull-out tray in front of him. His cell is charging, plugged into the outlet at his feet. He's got his earbuds in so he can listen to music while he writes.

All of it's this amazing technology. It's the present, but it's also so many signs of the future. If I think too much about it, I feel very small, and the world, beyond huge. I think about wandering and getting lost and how everyone should have their own north.

But right now I want to talk to you about shrines, okay? Old, traditional, and full-of-meaning shrines.

Do you know there are over ten thousand of them here in Japan?

I didn't. Neither did Shoma. But we looked it up, and it's true.

Some of them are huge and famous, and those are the ones the guidebooks usually tell you to go and see.

And some of them are just these tiny structures on the side of the road, tucked away between shops or houses. What you might miss if you blink or walk by too fast.

I almost missed this one today. It was nearly hidden from the street, just this small shrine in a local park we were passing on the way to the station.

But there were torii climbing out of the nearby trees, like the cattails that poke out of ditches along back roads. The orange of them against the green was as bright as emergency traffic cones.

Which means maybe that shrine had been looking out for me, Jory. Kannon and Mazu and Kwan Tai were around, and they told this shrine about a kid still trying to say sorry. It sensed the lucky cat from outside Shoma's place, and the cat's beckoning paw told it to watch for me. What else explains Shoma telling me afterward the orange hadn't been that bright at all? That the torii had barely been visible from where we'd been standing?

We were already late getting to the station, but I knew I had to visit that shrine before leaving Osaka. I just did. My feet kept going, and Shoma didn't even say anything as he followed, as though he knew I had to visit, too.

Going to Sensoji Temple the other day, I only went for my Summer Celebration Project. To find something for my topic of home and then write about it for Mr. Zaher. I'd expected souvenir booths and tourists and old buildings. As for stuff about gods and spirits, I wasn't going to be interested.

But then I bought some bad luck. And I tried to get rid of it. I was being chased by something invisible, something that's not supposed to be real, but still I felt it, at my back like a cold wind, an ugly shadow. I guess being in a place where things like fortune and power and kotodama are parts of everyday life, you can believe almost anything.

I don't know if that bad luck still follows me, and I didn't stop at this roadside shrine in Osaka because of it.

But I did stop for *some* kind of luck, it turns out.

Because even though they didn't sell omikuji there, they sold ema.

For five hundred yen, you write your wishes on the back of a small wooden plaque, and then you hang it at the shrine with all the other ema. Then you wait for a god to come along to read it and make it come true.

Most of the ema to choose from had drawings on the front, like geishas, or tidal waves, or samurai. But I bought a blank one. So I had both sides to write on.

I had a lot of things to wish for, Jory. To try to make right. Even gods can't fight science and turn back time, but I still had to try. I'll always keep trying, even if I've already hung up my ema for a kami to come along and read.

The words didn't come at first. I was full of wishes, but they were afraid to show themselves. In my head, they match up to what it's in my heart; but in ink, in words, I was afraid they wouldn't be enough. It's the same as how Perry freezes up during a shootout, how his hands of gold turn into concrete with all the pressure. His relief to get off the ice — we could always feel it from the bench as he skated by, remember?

Jory, that relief — I understand it, too. Now that I've decided hockey isn't for me. Not the way it is for you.

I'm really sorry for having taken it away. As though I've torn down your home, made it unsafe. And I'm beginning to know now how horrible it must be, to possibly lose it for good.

Here is what I eventually wrote on my ema. It's not as long as I thought it would be, needing to explain everything.

But I think it reads okay.

I think it gets down to what counts.

See you when I get back, all right?

Jory, I wish I were way better with words. The way good songwriters are, or Shoma and his interviews, how they're like invitations right into someone's brain, someone's heart. I wish this ema I'm writing on could be as powerful as Light's notebook in Death Note *except that it saves instead of dooms. So I'm sorry if all this ends up sounding stupid anyway.*

First of all, I wish for your eye to get better so

you can keep playing hockey. I wish that you'll jump right back into the game like you haven't missed out at all. I wish that it'll still be there for you, and built even stronger, a home that's sticking around. And if that doesn't happen, I'll still wish we could be friends again one day. Your buddy, Kaede

34

Dear Mom,

Here are some things that would make you happy to know, if you were here.

Shoma's not hiding who he is anymore.

Before I got here, he never talked about family. People he knows—bands, the stage crew and security guards at all the venues he's usually at—had no clue I even existed. They say he can talk to them for days about lives and music, but about us, not a word.

Last night, though, he introduced me to everyone we saw. He told them all I was from Canada and how I'm here for the rest of the summer. The way he said it, you never would have guessed he was only babysitting me until Dad came back. Which was cool.

One of the people he introduced me to was Eriko, the singer of the band who played last night. I know Shoma won't mind if I tell you I'm pretty sure he likes her a lot, and that she likes him that way back.

You'd also be happy to know that he's a pretty important guy when it comes to his work. He's found a place to fit.

At first, when I saw how he had this whole life outside

of the brother who'd gone silent on me, it made me mad. It was almost like he shouldn't have had the chance to succeed, not after disappearing. But now I see it differently. I see how he had to work really hard to push us out of his mind so he could be someone else, not be in the shadows of his half-ghost family. How he wasn't just the kid with a constantly missing dad, with a stepmom who decided he was okay without her, with a brother who didn't ask for him.

And about hockey . . . I'm not so sure it's really for me. I'll still play sometimes, but it'll just be for fun. I think I wanted it to mean something special to me, and when it didn't, I couldn't figure out how to start looking elsewhere.

This morning, me and Shoma were in a guitar shop, and he showed me how to play.

It wasn't as difficult as I thought it would be, Mom.

So I'm going to keep trying. Keep doing my best to learn how to play it for real, make it mine. I want to see if it'll become one of those parts that I can drop in that well Shoma says is home.

Playing shouldn't be about getting people to say you're the best, anyway, but to play just because you want to. Dad was never around to tell me I was doing okay, except I convinced myself I needed him there, just to believe I was.

When I get back to Canada and to school, I need to remember I can be okay whether he's around or not.

Home will be a really hard place for a while. But Grandpa will become less of a stranger over time. He's still too big on news radio all day long, so I'll work on getting him to switch up stations once in a while.

I texted Jory again, even though he's still not answering—asking about his eye, about him, saying I'm sorry and that I wish we can hang out again one day. His eye might never get better, Mom, but I'll keep hoping it will.

I'll eventually move on to junior high, though it might not happen this year.

And maybe, one day, the phone will ring. And it'll be Shoma calling.

35

I'm in my room, lying on my stomach on my futon and flipping through yet another magazine from my brother's collection. They're in piles all around me, like sandcastles grown tall around kids at a beach. Shoma's working at Rock in Japan tomorrow, and I'm reading about the festival out there in Ibaraki, trying to find a definition of home somewhere. Four days, hundreds of bands, thousands of people gathered together—there must be something in a year's worth of words (a lot of them my brother's).

Last night, after getting back from Osaka, I stared at the still-mostly-bare family tree section of my project and decided to lie.

Ms. Nanda would never know. Neither would Mr. Zaher. I'd tried not to think about how I promised him I'd really, really try. How leaving his office that last day of school, it was the first time since Mom's dying that the counselor hadn't had sad eyes saying good-bye to me.

Shoma had watched as I made up a family for us. I sat down in the front room and wrote down the names of strangers, picking them randomly from articles from the newspaper. He hadn't pointed out I was cheating. Instead he'd helped me create relatives, helped me invent whole branches of people who cared.

I have a feeling he's done this before.

So I'll make up for it with the rest of the project. I'll have to. I'll add more brochures, drag Shoma to more tourist sites, and save tickets stubs from lives we go to. Along with my journal entries, I'm going to believe I'll figure out home soon.

Only my dad's absence continues to gnaw, my box of questions still heavy.

I call him when I can, whenever Shoma's not going to notice. But nothing always answers, just that same void. And Sapporo is beginning to feel beyond far (according to an online dictionary, *far* is over a great distance, across much time), while Shoma's bass is just sitting here right in the closet, the very definition of *near* (at hand, soon, immediate).

This time, the dictionary seems to have it right.

I flip through more magazines—if my brain's too busy reading, it can't keep going back and forth, telling me to choose.

Sapporo or Tokyo.

Dad or Shoma.

Answers to old questions, or new memories made. Hurt now or hurt later.

Pages suddenly drift out of the magazine I'm reading. They spin their way onto the tatami mats beside the futon, landing with a swish.

I lean over and pick them up. They've been sliced out from a different magazine and then saved between the pages of this other one. My mom had done something like this, cutting out recipes from magazines and papers to try one day. She kept them all in a binder above the stove, never remembering to look at them again.

At first I think it's one of Shoma's articles, or something he's saved for reference.

It's supposed to be anything but what it is.

A reporter's print interview with Tsubasa Hirano. It's from a Japanese photography magazine. The date on the corner says it was published nearly three years ago, fall 2012.

My stomach (which has been feeling more than fine lately) begins to ache as I read about our dad's plans to leave us:

> *His voice is full of energy over the phone, despite the fact that for the past two months, he's been living in a tent in the middle of a forest.*
>
> *"Rest is going to have to wait," Hirano declares. "I already need to be back out there, somewhere, wherever that might be. Whatever place or subject wants me next. The world's a big place, too big to fit into my apartment. Which means going out there to see it."*

And then:

> *Anyone who knows the photographer also knows he hates staying still. Rest? Routine? Home? Hirano says he and such words aren't a healthy fit.*

His laugh is a boom through the phone, excited
for a future still to be imagined. "The next time I'm
gone, it could be anywhere from a month to six,
from a year to five. It could be anywhere in the
world. Whatever decides to call me, I'm listening."

My pulse is a drum, beating hard in my ears.

Five years?

Dad would have been okay being gone that long? Not even okay but *excited*?

I wish I could believe my kanji is bad enough that I'm reading the clipping wrong, but I know it isn't. Mom had been so careful checking it during those years at our kitchen table, the language one of the few things about Japan she hadn't let herself leave behind.

Shoma had probably saved the interview to read a bunch of times, trying to believe it.

Or, maybe, trying *not* to. He wouldn't have been a kid anymore, and Dad would have already been mostly missing.

But . . . kids are supposed to stay kids to their folks forever, aren't they? Gemma's parents always say this to her older sisters, whenever they talk about moving out and finally being independent. Her folks tease they'll call all the time to check, to make surprise visits and always be close by. They promise to never forget about their kids.

Three years ago, I wouldn't have been around for our dad to ditch and disappoint.

Only Shoma would have been.

My stomach swims, and I feel sick for my brother.

If I'm ever a dad, I'm never going anywhere. I'll stick to my kids like the world's strongest Krazy Glue. I'll be the most annoying and clingy dad ever.

Still holding the clipping, I leave the room to find Shoma.

I want to know where Dad went after the article was published. How long he ended up staying away. If he came home afterward and actually stayed for a while, wanting to catch up with his oldest son. Or if he only came back to do more interviews, each about disappearing for even longer, before taking off again. *Six years, kids! Seven! Let's just make it ten so we can call it the Decade of Dad!*

So many questions, all spilling out of that small box.

With only my brother around to answer them.

36

There's a gyoza-eating contest happening on the television, and the stereo's turned up loud and playing something with lots of bass.

Shoma's in the kitchen, his head deep in the fridge.

I want to tell him there's no food in there, but before I can, he's already shut it, looking uncertainly at the packages he's holding. It's the same hamburg steak and kimchi from before, when I first got here.

"I wouldn't eat those if I were you," I tell him.

He glances up, mock scowling. "Expiry dates don't mean much."

"Or they can mean a lot."

He laughs and sets the food down on the counter. "How's the research going? Find anything you can use for your project?"

"Some stuff, yeah." I hold out the clipping. "Shoma, I found this in one of the magazines. It's an interview with Dad."

My brother takes it. His face changes as he begins to read. From confusion to impatience to being tired. He hands it back before I know he's done, and by then his face shows nothing. "Yeah, I remember this. What about it?"

"You didn't finish reading it."

"I read it a long time ago, Kaede. I don't need to read it again." He carefully opens the container of hamburg and sniffs it. "I'm going to run to the konbini and grab something. Want to come along?"

"I'm still full from dinner. Hey, this interview—Dad says he wouldn't mind going away for as long as five years." Saying it out loud doesn't make it seem more reasonable, doesn't shrink down time.

My brother shrugs and tosses the hamburg into the garbage. "Like I've said, Dad's Dad. The disappearing act is second nature to him."

"It's from three years ago. Haven't you ever asked him about it?"

"Ask him what?"

"Whether or not he meant it."

Shoma shrugs again, and now he's dumping out the leftover kimchi. "There wouldn't have been any point to ask. Him saying it is him meaning it."

My fingers are colder than they should be as I place the clipping on the kitchen counter. "Didn't you want him to *not* mean it?"

Shoma's face has a bit of the coldness that's in my fingers. Even his blue hair manages to look nearly unfriendly, the blue more of deep ice than the sky. "I don't think Dad really cares what either of us want when it comes to his work."

"So after you read it, you just . . . left it?"

"Even if I'd asked him, it would have been the same answer he's always given. He goes where the work goes."

"But—" I look at Shoma, sad for the kid he'd been, the kid that's crept back into his eyes, turning his voice funny again. "You'd still be here."

"That's never mattered. Look, I'm hungry, and I don't want to talk about Dad anymore. Let's go. I'll buy you something."

"You kept the interview, though. It must have bugged you."

Shoma picks up the clipping and drops it into the recycling bin. His expression is grim and angry, full of thunder and clouds. It's too close to how a lot of people have looked at me lately. "Talking about the past isn't going to make him come back any faster. You know Dad. You know what he's like."

Suddenly I'm more mad than upset, maybe even as mad as he is. "*You* might know what he's like, but I don't. How can I?"

"Actually, him not being here is how you know," Shoma says quietly. "Better get used to it."

My eyes tear up, so my brother becomes a huge, messy blur. "He'll be here soon."

The sight of me starting to cry makes him go still, and quiet. Just the way he did on the train, when he said he was trying to be a better brother.

He sighs like he's never been more exhausted, then reaches over and roughly scrubs his knuckles over my hair.

"I really hope so, Kaede," he says, his voice all gentle now, and I wish he'd stay mad so I could. "And I'm sorry, I didn't mean to upset you. But you know, it's the truth. Finding that old article changes nothing. We'll go to the festival tomorrow, we'll finish your project, and we'll still have lots of time to hang out afterward before you go home."

I nod, my neck stiff, blinking hard.

I can tell his *we* doesn't include Dad.

"You okay now?" Shoma's still feeling bad. His eyes are dark with it.

I nod again, not okay at all. It's gotten hard to take a deep breath. That box of questions suddenly feels too heavy to wait any longer. It's starting to sink my whole boat. Water's coming in over the top so there's a waterfall right at my feet. I can't bail fast enough.

Shoma would never understand to help. He once had his own box of tough questions for our dad, and the answers he got weren't good enough. Why would he care that I still had mine to ask?

And just like that, I make up my mind.

For days I'd been stuck, lost because of it. I'd gone back and forth like a compass with a broken needle, the direction north no longer a sure thing. Like Mom's radio sometimes getting caught between stations, so she had to jiggle the dial to make it decide.

"You sure you don't want to come with me to the store?" Shoma's gaze stays watchful, uncertain. "There's mochi ice cream."

I shake my head. My stomach's twisting, and a weird hollowness has taken over my brain, just like the dead air that came between those radio stations. "I'm going to go to bed, since we have to catch the train so early in the morning."

"Right, we do." He can't hide his relief to talk about something safe, something he knows—little brothers, ones who come with too much baggage, are neither. "Don't forget to set the alarm on your cell."

Back in my room, I call my dad, my fingers still cold as they dial.

His voice mail picks up this time. I'm so surprised I nearly start talking, reveal to him my plans. But then I realize he might call Shoma and get him to stop me.

I disconnect, turn off the light, and crawl into bed. I stare at the ceiling, waiting. The streetlamp outside flickers its glow into the room through the blinds, and once in a while cars drive down the street so pavement crunches. Between crunches my heart thuds and thuds.

There are no sounds from inside the apartment, though, no signs of Shoma finally leaving for the konbini. I guess he's forgotten about being hungry. Or maybe he's got a tornado in his stomach, too, the other half of mine.

When I think he's finally asleep, I roll off the futon. Using the flashlight on my cell so I can see not to miss any of my stuff, I begin to pack.

37

It's past midnight when I crack open my door and step out of my room to check.

Like I'd guessed, the rest of the apartment's gone quiet, the TV and stereo turned off and in the dark. No light peeks out from beneath Shoma's door. The silence is weird, turning the place unfamiliar. Shoma not still being awake is also weird—it's the first time since I've been here that he's gone to sleep before me.

I go back into my room and head for the closet. Still holding my cell as a flashlight, I pull open the door. I do it while barely breathing, while trying not to think. My throat's tight with nerves, my stomach all wound up.

Shoma's bass is cold in my hand as I grab it from behind the jackets and boxes. It's heavier than the guitar I'd played at Frets. I pull out the amp, too—a set would sell for more, I bet.

The lucky cat beckons from the ground as I lock the outer door behind me, its ceramic paw a slow and steady sweep of white. It smiles at me the way it always does, like I'm not making plans to run away and betray Shoma. The tiny path is empty around us, the acupuncture clinic next door closed until tomorrow.

I don't have any five-yen coins on me, but even if I did,

I don't know what I'd wish for. How do you ask for something to be fixed when you're the one who's deciding to mess it up? How do you wonder about a choice when it's the only one you can make?

"Give me a sign of what to do," I whisper to the lucky cat, my voice somehow still too loud in the quiet. It's all shaky, too, just like a little kid's after getting caught in a lie.

Because . . . why do I still feel lost, if I know what I need to do?

What good are things like kotodama and omikuji and ema if I'm still confused?

Where have Kannon and Mazu and Kwan Tai gone?

The cat just waves and waves, as silent as those gods.

"It's okay," I whisper again. I throw the strap of Shoma's bass over my shoulder, hug the amp to my chest, and move down the path. "I'd save your luck for someone else, too."

Shinjuku is just as it was the last time I was out so late— still crowded, full of people and noise and music. The air smells of food and cigarette smoke. I pass by the same konbini where I'd eaten middle-of-the-night curry and spaghetti-flavored chips. The one where the cashier was mistaken and thought I belonged.

It's Kabukicho that's different this time.

When I'd gone before, it'd already gone to sleep. Now it's just waking up, and as I get closer to the district's center, the streets slowly change. There are bits of glass and plastic on the pavement, collections of grime in the corners of shop windows. Lights are either too bright or too dim so there are shadows everywhere. Faces wear too much makeup, and the laughter that rings out is full of odd, shrill edges.

During that outdoor education class trip last year, the week we'd slept under the stars, we'd also slept next to forests. And it was at night that those forests sometimes felt different. Not dangerous, just more mysterious. As though when we fell asleep, the trees woke up for real and began to talk to each other.

Kabukicho is Shinjuku, but it's also not.

I swallow hard and pull Shoma's bass closer. I hug his amp closer, too, my arms clamped tight around it. Both are my way to my dad, but if I were in the ocean right now and holding them just this way, their weight would sink me. The same way my box of questions wants to sink me.

I don't know what to think about that.

Maybe my quest for answers is doomed from the start.

Maybe it means I should probably come in from the water completely.

I keep walking. No one stops me. Looks that come my way don't last long. A part of me wants to call out, make someone notice. So they can turn me around and make me go back to Shoma's, my plan ruined just in time.

But I stay quiet, and I'm left alone. I move even faster now, following the directions on my cell. Shoma's bass feels heavier than it did when I left the apartment, like it's trying to pull me back. To remind me it's more than steel and strings. That it still has songs for me to hear, if only I stay.

The third resale shop on my list is still open because it

happens to share the space with a twenty-four-hour ticket reseller. Just like at Frets, there are guitars displayed in the windows. But there's junk, too, a lot of it ugly and useless, and my hand twists the strap of my brother's bass. I picture Shoma showing me how to press down on the frets, as patient as Mom had been when she'd taught me what she'd held on to.

In the end, it's easy to hand it over, way easier than it should be. It makes me wonder how many other kids come in way past midnight to sell a bass to find their missing dads. Then I stop wondering because there's only one possible answer, and my eyes get hot when Mom's voice fills my head. *Kaede, it's not too late to go back. Shoma might have given up on Dad, but he hasn't given up on you.*

"Ten thousand, five hundred yen," the lady from behind the counter says, her voice swallowing up Mom's. "For the set. Happy with that?"

I nod, unsure how I feel. She hands me the bills. They're slick in my fingers.

I head over to the nearest konbini with an ATM and take out all the money on my grandpa's emergency money card. Twenty thousand more yen. This money feels too slick, too.

I don't find out until I'm back at Shinjuku Station that you can't swap out Suica fare cards for their balance in cash. I hadn't counted on that.

It leaves me eight thousand yen short of a train fare and plane ride to Sapporo.

But then I remember how I still have Shoma's credit card.

From when I went out by myself and he'd been worried, the way a dad might be.

Just in case, my brother had said. *For things you think you really need.*

I'd lied to him that day, too.

Before my mom's voice can come back and chime in with his, I'm rushing toward one of the ticket kiosks.

I punch the information into the screen. Using my cash, I book a seat on a train that leaves from Shinjuku Station tomorrow morning. Then I go online and use my cell to buy a plane ticket from Tokyo to Sapporo, charging it to Shoma's card.

The whole time something in my chest pushes and pulls, a broken compass's needle spinning and spinning.

A town could be blown away by the wind battering around in my stomach.

Cities, even.

Whole entire *countries*.

I leave the station, pretty sure that buying stuff for running away should be even *harder* than selling stuff to do it. Not easier.

I half run along the still-crowded sidewalk, working out in my head the rest of how I'm going to leave my brother behind. Faces blur, my eyes hotter than ever.

If I leave the festival as soon as Shoma heads off to his stage to work, I should be able to make it back here in time. Before getting on the train I'll stop at his place to pick up my stuff (being caught again with a full backpack for a day trip would only be suspicious), and then I'll leave his apartment key with the staff at Irusu. I'll be at Haneda Airport by noon tomorrow, in Sapporo by four in the afternoon.

I don't want to imagine Shoma's face when he realizes I've left.

How I'd chosen, over him, our wandering dad and my useless questions and my stupid need for answers.

Now I'm running for real, dodging and weaving around people who don't have to, who have a place of their own. The missing weight of Shoma's bass and amp is huge, and I guess it's what guilt feels like. I run all the way back to the apartment, my lungs burning, my whole stomach a hurricane.

38

Dear Kaede,

How nice it is to hear from you! I hope you're enjoying Japan and discovering all kinds of new things.

After speaking to Ms. Nanda, we're both fine with not including your Summer Celebration Project for the lobby display. We know some things can be too personal to want to share, meant more for you than anyone else. We just need to be confident that you understand the spirit of the project and see how effectively you've applied yourself to your selected theme.

Good luck with everything,

Mr. Zaher

39

It's ten in the morning, and this part of the world is on fire.

I pluck at the front of my T-shirt, pretty certain all my sunscreen has already melted away, and glance back at the main entrance gates.

A huge sea of people is rolling inward, shimmering beneath the sun. It's Shinjuku Station times one hundred, its close walls and ceilings torn away to make even more room. There's an energy in the air, too, like lightning about to happen. I think of the old beehive in my backyard, its swarm of busy occupants spilled out all at once so their buzzing was everywhere. I'd felt the sound along the skin of my arms, the same way the festival's energy dances off it now.

I bet storm chasers feel something like this. As though they've been painted with a current of electricity, the certainty that something's about to happen.

Shoma checks the fit of my attendance wristband to make sure it's not too loose. If I lose it, there go my in-and-out privileges.

Not that it matters, since I won't need it for more than a few minutes.

He glances down at his cell to check the time, the crowd flowing in all around us. "Okay, Kaede, I have to go sign in—the first shows are scheduled to start pretty soon. So, rules:

be careful with your wristband, don't get too close to the front of the crowds or you'll get crushed, keep slathering on the sunscreen, and make sure you come find me in time later tonight. Sound good?"

"I'll make sure." Guilt churns me up, crawls around my stomach. One of those storm watchers would take a single look at me and know what's brewing inside. "Lake Stage, 6:40 P.M." Nothing's Carved In Stone, the band my brother wants us to watch together.

"Text me if you need anything before then. It might take me a bit if I'm in the middle of something, but I *will* text you back."

He's thinking about Dad. How he's not him. Reminding me how different they are.

I want to tell him he can stop worrying about me thinking that. I did once, lumping them together as one and the same after they turned faceless and into just outlines, a tag team of two strangers. I could tell him, make him happy, tell myself he can think back to it later, after he finds out what I needed to do and is no longer so happy.

But my brother's no longer a stranger, and I don't think I can erase him away now, even if I tried.

"Okay, I will." I'm glad I'm wearing sunglasses so Shoma can't see so much. My ribs ache holding back what's gone heavy in my chest, the heart in there that's a giant bruise.

"Cool," he says, smiling.

Shoma had cried the day we'd left, Mom had told me a long time ago. Her voice had cracked as she'd said it, had ground down to a whisper. *I was so sorry to leave him, Kaede. He was so hurt. It's still the hardest thing I've ever done, leaving him alone like that.*

The questions I would ask her if she were still here:

How do you say good-bye without it sounding like good-bye? To say thank you for a week where so much happened it was like living another person's life, the half of me I haven't been since I was three? To say thank you for being a brother, when Shoma could have just stayed away? For showing me how home isn't the single dull definition the dictionary says it is, but something way more complex and interesting and real?

"Shoma?"

"Yeah?" He's checking his cell again. His life, keeping him busy, one he built all on his own.

"I— Thanks for all the help. With my school project and ... all of it. I think you made it a lot better than it would have been." I blink fast behind my sunglasses, willing the tears back and not doing a good job. "Really. I mean it."

My brother's grin goes wide. The blue of his hair shines, a streak of sky. Ripped black jeans, tattoos, his earrings bright in the sun.

He doesn't look any different since the first time I saw him, there at the airport for me, making up for our missing dad.

Except that he does.

The thing is, I know it's because he looks like family now.

Shoma scrubs at my hair with a hand, gives me a super

quick one-armed hug, and then he's gone without another word.

I can't talk anymore, either.

I turn back the way I came and begin to run—as though I'm being chased, a huge storm about to happen.

When *I'm* supposed to be doing the chasing.

40

The plane lands in Chitose Airport in Hokkaido more than five hours later, at three in the afternoon.

My stomach hits the ground along with the landing gear. The flight attendant is saying something about staying seated until the plane's completely stopped moving. Somewhere in the cabin, a baby cries. Passengers are restless, tugging at their seat belts, turning airplane mode off on their cells and getting back online to check their emails and texts.

I stare out the window, suddenly nervous about more than just seeing my dad for the first time in nearly a decade. It's my first time being in this part of Japan, so far north from Tokyo. I don't know much about Hokkaido except that it's the second biggest of the four islands that make up the country. And it's got real winters, with months and months of snow.

It's also got mountains, ones remote enough to keep a dad in hiding.

The same way a ghost might hide.

I still don't know how to find him. My plans end once I get to Sapporo Station.

But there are only four accessible mountains in

Hokkaido's capital city, and only a dozen or so bed-and-breakfasts. And my dad is Tsubasa Hirano, famous photographer—it's not his first time here. Owners and staff would know his face, his name. How hard can it be to track him down?

I'd never gotten details from Shoma about where our dad was staying, even though my brother had reminded me to bug him. And by the time I knew I needed to, asking would have been suspicious.

I wonder what band he's watching right now. If he's tried to find me despite working, despite my assuring him I was fine. If he's noticed I'm gone from the festival altogether. If he believes my leaving is because of something he did.

That's what bothers me the most. Him feeling bad when all he's supposed to be is relieved I'm no longer his responsibility.

Before the plane took off, I'd sent him a single text from the airport, just to keep him from worrying until I could call him after landing:

Don't want to bug you while you work, so I'll just hang out until tonight. See you at Lake Stage for Nothing's Carved In Stone!

Moments later: *Okay, see you then. And it's way too hot out, so eat lots of kakigori!*

The plane finally rolls to a complete stop, and passengers get out of their seats, reach overhead for their luggage.

I'm inside the airport terminal, walking alongside a small food court, when I get back online.

A bunch of texts come through all at once.

All from Shoma. All asking where I am. All sounding worried.

Guilt twists me up, and I'm about to call him when my cell rings in my hand.

"Hello?" I say into it without looking at the number, sure it's my brother.

"Kaede?" my dad asks.

41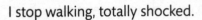

I stop walking, totally shocked.

"Dad?"

"Kaede, you called? I'm dialing my last missed one."

My father's voice is faint over my cell, but I still recognize it. Voices are their own memory. I'd remembered Shoma's, too.

"I did call," I say stupidly, hating how young I suddenly sound. A strange kind of whooshing noise fills my ears, coming and going with my pulse. If I'm so surprised, I wonder how my dad must have reacted, seeing my cell number show up on his. He's been in my head for years, but me in his? How *not* on his mind have I been?

"Are things all right?" he asks. "What's the emergency?"

I didn't know there had to be one. My mouth is slow to move, the same way my feet still aren't moving, even though people are swerving around me, buying snacks or rushing for a gate or for the exit.

"You still there, Kaede?" A note of impatience creeps into the sound of my name.

"I'm here, Dad," I say, my face flushing. "In Japan. In Hokkaido."

"Hokkaido? Why?"

"I came to meet up with you."

"But I'm not in Hokkaido. I'm in New Zealand."

More shock.

New Zealand?

I don't know anything about New Zealand except that it's also far away from Tokyo.

"But Shoma said you were here. Right now." My Japanese comes out in awkward, broken-up fragments, no longer easy for me.

"Well, I *was* in Hokkaido—Sapporo—last year. But now I'm in New Zealand."

Last year.

My dad's been gone from Tokyo since then? Maybe even since that article that Shoma's saved, the one where my dad talks about no limits? *The next time I'm gone, it could be anywhere from a month to six, from a year to five.*

"I thought I told your brother the last time we spoke that I would head out here directly this time, instead of stopping by home between shoots like I usually do. But I can't be sure, I might have meant to but forgot. Either way, it's been a bit since I've been in touch. And reception here is mostly terrible—if Shoma's tried to reach me, I'm afraid it never got through."

It's been a bit since I've been in touch.

The last time I heard from my dad was an email, when I'd been eight. I'd read the final line over and over again, because it was supposed to be a promise. *I'll talk to you in a bit, Kaede, all right?*

I guess we both have different ideas what *a bit* means.

"Kaede, why aren't you at home?"

Home.

The word has grown oversized. No definition can possibly contain it. It's like the world, stuffed into four letters.

Hearing it from my dad—just what did it mean to him, anyway?

"You asked me to come, Dad, remember? Last week. To come and stay with you for the rest of the summer, you said. Shoma passed on your message. But I got tired of waiting in Tokyo, so here I am."

My dad's surprise jumps from his cell and into mine. It comes at me like a punch.

"I haven't been home for nearly two years." His words are very careful, like he's not sure how I'm taking whatever he's saying. "I don't know why your brother would tell you that. But it's fine, I'm glad you're visiting. Is Shoma with you in Hokkaido?"

I stare at the crowd rushing all around me, at the way everyone's mouths move as they talk and laugh. But I don't hear any of it. I don't even hear my dad as he keeps asking me about my vacation.

My brain scrambles to understand. Parts are working and wheeling away, trying so hard.

Why would Shoma not tell me about our dad being gone this whole time? And then lie about who asked me to come?

Somersaults are happening in my stomach. Flips and dives, huge leaps off giant springboards.

"Unfortunately"—Dad's still talking, but I'm barely listening—"I'm not going to make it back to Japan anytime soon. My contract says I have to stay put until the shoot's done. Unless it's a family emergency, but I don't think this really qualifies—Shoma's there, after all."

My brother was the one who'd been around to first hear the news about Mom. He's the one who asked how I was after she died. He's the one who managed to meet me at the airport.

"I'm still sorry it took me so long going through my messages to hear about your mother. By the time I could use my cell again, it'd been weeks, nearly two months, and— well, I wasn't sure your grandpa needed to hear from me by that point. I assumed Shoma had talked to him, and I knew he'd take care of everything and would do his best to be there for you."

Anger's growing inside my chest, sharp little spikes trying to climb my throat.

Because Shoma's also the one who said he was passing on our messages to our dad, when he wasn't. He asked me to come visit and let me think it was Dad trying to make things better. When really it was just him wanting to do something to stop feeling guilty.

He keeps telling me to get over Dad and to not bother trying to reach him.

He's still covering for him now, that's why he's been lying about him being away. A tag team of two, as I always knew.

"Dad, I have to go." My voice sounds nearly like Shoma's

when he gets upset. I'm struggling not to cry even as my insides sting. I feel the way I did biking to Mr. Ames's house, the way I did skating up behind Jory. "Shoma's calling for me."

"Sure, okay." He must not notice that I'm upset because all I hear in *his* voice is relief. "I'll talk to you both soon, all right, Kaede? In a bit."

"Right. Okay, bye." I hang up and start walking through the terminal, though I don't know where I'm going, who to find.

It's like I've dumped that old box of questions right over the side of the boat and replaced it with a brand-new one. It's even harder to row now, and I think I'm going to sink, once and for all.

This box has questions, too, but they're not about the past, and they're not for my dad.

Shoma, my big brother, taking care of everything.

I keep going—through halls and shops, up escalators and then back down them—as though I'm still trying to leave behind that bad luck omikuji. As though it's not already too late.

And Kannon, the Goddess of Mercy, the one who's supposed to be kind?

I guess she's just as lost as me, since I can't sense her at all.

42

I'm at the airport in Hokkaido.

I know you've been lying about Dad.

I have all my things, and money for a ticket, so I'm just going to fly home.

43

Wait for me there.
I'm catching the first plane out.

44

Shoma comes flying around into my section of the terminal, his eyes wide and searching, his blue hair wild. There's a festival press pass around his neck, and the sight of his wrist-band reminds me I'm still wearing mine. It'd stuck around, after all.

"Kaede!"

My brother's yell is a boom, echoing along the rows of empty chairs. It's past midnight, and this part of the terminal is deserted. Outside, the sky is nearly black but for the watchful moon, and our reflections show on the huge glass windows: Shoma swooping fast in my direction like he's trying to catch something, and me in my chair, legs crossed, backpack in my lap, stuck.

Shoma reaches me, and for a long second he's absolutely still, as though he can't decide if he's supposed to be angry or relieved. Then he just collapses into the empty seat next to me and slides low enough he's practically lying down.

It's nearly six hours to get from the festival grounds in Chiba to Hokkaido.

He really did have to race over, the same way I had. And he'd been working, too. He's missed hours of shows, of music. He's missed watching Nothing's Carved In Stone.

"What are you doing, Kaede?" My brother asks this so

quietly I can barely hear him in the already silent room. He slowly sits up. "Seriously."

"I wanted to see Dad." The words are somehow too simple, even if they're the truth. "But you lied about him being here in Hokkaido."

"I never lied. He is here. At least, he *was* here, the last time we talked."

"He's in New Zealand."

"What?" His surprise is too real to be fake. He probably would have reacted the same if I'd said Mars, or the moon (from Japan, New Zealand's twelve hours away by air, I'd checked). "Who told you this?"

"Dad did. He finally called me back today."

Shoma sighs and rubs his face. "You've been calling him this whole time, haven't you?"

"He says he's been there since last year." Fresh tears sting my eyes. "A whole year! Why'd you lie?"

My brother's shaking his head. His eyes have the same sad look as Mr. Zaher's. "I didn't know, Kaede. I swear. His cell never worked when he was in Sapporo two years ago, so one day I just . . . stopped calling. It's routine for him, going away for weeks, then boom, suddenly being back in town. Only this time, I guess he never bothered coming home again before leaving for his next job."

I can tell he so badly wants me to believe him. A part of me wants to.

But what if he's lying because he doesn't want to admit

how our dad has ditched him, too? What if it's because he's decided it's *my* turn to be tricked, now that I'm here?

"You made up him wanting me to visit." There are planes in the sky outside, their lights blinking and winking. I wonder if they're coming or going, how often they get to just stay on the ground. "It's not a game. I'm not a joke."

"You're not at all." Shoma appears cornered and wary and kind of helpless. "Look, talking to your grandpa, I knew you were in trouble. And your mom had just died—I didn't want to tell you about Dad not being here, too. And . . . I didn't think you'd come if it was just me asking. We didn't even know each other, brothers or not."

"And now you're trying to make up for it, hanging out with me, pretending you don't mind." My face is wet, but I just leave it.

"I *like* hanging out with you, Kaede."

"I don't believe you." Trusting him is dangerous. Why haven't I learned that yet? "You just needed proof that you're not the only one Dad's forgotten, and that's why you asked me to come."

"Of course not."

"Then was it punishment for me and Mom leaving you, too?"

Shoma's whole face goes tight. I bet a minute passes before he speaks again. And his voice, as it always is when he's upset, is rough and sore sounding, full of hurts.

"Listen. When you and your mom left, I lost my family,

all right? I had to go back to living with someone who always wanted to be anywhere else. So, yes, maybe I *did* hate you and your mom for leaving, just a bit, and that's the truth. And I admit I knew I was ignoring you all these years, okay?" He's picking at the threads on his jeans, staring hard at them, the way I'm careful to stare hard at things that can't stare back. "I was so sorry to hear about your mom. But at least you have your grandpa, Kaede, and at least he cares to try. You're actually luckier than you know."

Each of his words is like one of those chisels artists use, chipping away at their project, getting to the heart of it.

Shoma still has a project of his own, just as I do.

This whole time, we've been working on the same thing. Our own tag team.

"I'm sorry we made you hate us," I whisper. Mom would want me to make sure he knows. "We should have tried harder, too."

His smile still isn't all the way in his eyes. "And I should have been more careful about Dad being here. I just figured everything would somehow work out, even if you had to leave before he came back. I thought you'd be okay with it in the end, because you would have had fun anyway. Because maybe I would have been enough."

"I've been having a great time. I don't want to leave." I swipe my sleeve across my face and give him a small grin. "You're kind of supposed to be a jerk, you know?"

"Sorry." Now he laughs, the real thing.

"And . . . you're not kidding about liking hanging out,

right?" Somewhere unseen in the terminal, someone's running a vacuum.

"Not kidding in the least." His face gets serious. "I really do hope you get to see Dad before you have to leave."

"Me too." But I already know I won't. I'd heard it in our dad's voice over my cell, how he couldn't hide it. The eagerness to get away, to get back to what is *his* home. "Shoma, about that interview I found—why did you save it?"

He shrugs. "After his Hokkaido shoot finished, I tried to find out where he'd gone next. Or if he even ended up staying. That interview was the last print one I found—I stopped looking afterward." Shoma's still serious as he watches me. "He really never did call to let me know he'd moved on, Kaede."

"I know, I believe you." And I do.

A new silence forms, but it's a good one. Like a storm's just passed through and gotten rid of all the bad stuff that's been hanging on.

Speaking of bad stuff.

I might as well tell him now.

"Shoma, I sold your bass." I say it fast, the same way you're supposed to tear off bandages so they don't hurt (they still do). "The one you kept in the closet of my room. I used the money I got for it and then your credit card to help me buy my train and airplane tickets to Sapporo."

My brother blinks. "Wow, okay. That's . . . some planning, all right."

"I'm sorry."

"That was my very first bass, the one I taught myself to play on. I bought it with money I earned selling ice cream at Tokyo Sea. It was pretty much the worst summer job in the world."

I hunch farther into my chair. "I'm really, really sorry. I'll make it up to you."

Shoma only laughs again. "Just promise you won't take off on me the rest of the time you're here, and we'll call it even."

"Deal."

45

Dear Nothing's Carved In Stone,

It was my fault we missed you guys at RIJF.

But Shoma somehow got himself assigned to the Rising Sun Rock festival a week later. It was at RSR that that photo of Shinichi and Takeshi still being friends was taken, showing me that not all broken things are actually broken.

Flying to Hokkaido was more fun this time around, me and Shoma getting to go together.

He watched you guys play from nearer to the front, something he likes to do for all the shows he writes about. He says he likes to feel a live as best he can, as well as see and hear. For him, that's up close.

I stayed along the side, watching you as the crowd watches you, their faces telling me about home.

How it can be a field with room for thousands.

A stage for four.

The strange and cool and bright energy that is a song.

Really, it's that home is something inside of you. So you're never lost wherever you go in the world. You take it with you.

I'm almost done with my Summer Celebration Project.

I'm pretty happy with how it's turned out. I don't even

mind my mostly-made-up family tree that much, since me and Shoma worked on it together. It won't be the most well-done project in class, or the one that looks the best, or the most educational, but I believe it's true, and honest. Maybe those things will come close to Mr. Zaher's "truly excellent."

Ms. Nanda says we can use whatever fits in a notebook.

And Shoma didn't give me your music thinking it'd help me define home. But it has.

Which is why I'm going to include the lyrics to one of your songs.

It's one that knows me well, because I can find myself in the words. It's just as Shoma says: *Home is made up of those things I know will always be there for me.*

So don't stop writing songs or playing music. Because what "November 15th" means to me might be some other song for some other kid that's still inside of you. What you still need to write.

46

Hi, Mr. Zaher,

It's Kaede from school again.

I wanted to show you some pictures I've taken of my Summer Celebration Project. I know you and Ms. Nanda will still want to see the real thing next week after I get back, but maybe you can give me an idea of how it looks so far? That way, if I've somehow done it wrong, I'll still have time to fix it.

Thanks! (I'm attaching the photos to this email!)

Kaede

47

Dear Kaede,

Such a pleasure to see these photos of your work! Thank you very much for sending them along. The heart you've put into your Summer Celebration Project clearly shines through, and I'm very eager to see the rest upon your return.

While you are correct that Ms. Nanda and I will still need to assess the actual project, I can tell you I'm more than excited about your upcoming school year and what it means for you.

I think it's safe to say you should be excited, too.

Do enjoy the rest of your summer. Japan is beautiful, and now I mean to visit one day.

For that—and for sharing what promises to be a truly excellent project—thank you, Kaede.

Mr. Zaher

48

"So you remembered everything, right?" Shoma eyes my stuffed backpack. "Not that you have any room left in that thing."

I pat the outside of it. "It's okay, I've got it all."

I hadn't expected to be taking so much back to Canada with me. I'd even meant to leave things *behind*, even if those things were more weight than shape—a family I didn't need anymore, that box of tough questions for my dad.

But Shoma had given me small things over the weeks to take home, to keep us connected over the ocean. Things that had made him think of me when he saw them—a RSR keychain, a bright neon guitar pick, toys from capsule machines. Handed over really casually, so it wouldn't seem a big deal to either of us if I turned them away.

I never did.

Most of the time, I know I'll be okay, seeing all of that in my room in Vancouver. I'm no longer three but twelve— stronger now. So when Shoma slowly disappears on me, memories will make me happy instead of sad. I'll be able to imagine him getting back to his life here, exactly how it'd been before I came, and know that we're still brothers.

I'm luckier than I know.

Dad hasn't made it back to Tokyo, but my questions for

him haven't resurfaced. They're still deep in the water, after I threw them over the edge of my imaginary boat into my imaginary lake. Instead I got answers from Shoma, ones I hadn't known I needed. And those are just as good as ones I might have gotten from Dad. They make those questions not really matter anymore.

My Summer Celebration Project ended up being bigger than I ever would have guessed—it seems I had more to say on the topic of home than I thought. I was careful packing it this morning at Shoma's, this notebook thick with tickets and photos and writing, with everything else that felt right.

School starts in three days; I find out for sure in two if I'll be in Grade 7 or 8. I know what I'm hoping for—what I'm not so scared to hope for anymore—but I also think I'll be ready if the other happens.

I have souvenirs, too. For Gemma and Jory and other friends, and for Grandpa. I even got a small lucky cat for Mr. Zaher. I'm pretty sure he'll like it, especially after I tell him what it means, how he's supposed to leave it by his office door for whatever kids might walk through.

And Jory texted me back this past week. To tell me his eye is starting to see light again, that he wants to hang out after I'm back so he can hear about my trip. So I'm seeing him tomorrow. We're meeting up with Gemma and Roan and Donovan. It'll almost be just like old times again.

The lines at security are already long by the time we get

there. Laptops and briefcases and purses ride through scanners; guards wave passengers through.

Me and Shoma stop outside the last set of doors. This is as far as he can go.

"I hope the flight's not too bad," Shoma says. "Nine hours, right? Quicker this direction, at least."

It is. It takes more than ten the other way, because of the wind.

I nod. There's a lump in my throat I'm trying to pretend doesn't exist. "Yeah, but there'll be movies, and I've got tons of music on my cell now. It'll feel quick."

"Text me when you land just so I know you didn't end up flying into some other dimension?"

"Sure."

"Cool."

But Shoma doesn't give my head a final scrub with his knuckles, and he doesn't move to leave. Instead, he's fiddling with the cap of his bottle of tea, suddenly seeming nervous. He's not saying any of the things I thought he would, either, things that are supposed to make our good-bye easier, to feel not as permanent as it probably, most likely, is.

I hope you don't fail.

Keep up with guitar lessons.

Text if you want.

"Kaede, I'm wondering, how would you feel about moving back to Japan?"

I stare at my brother. "What?"

"Well, you'd just go to school here, the same as you would in Vancouver." Shoma's still fiddling, but then he gives me a grin. "Your Japanese is good enough that you won't be behind for long. You already have a room at my place. We'll get ahold of Dad again for money for stuff you'll eventually need, but if we can't, we'll still figure something out."

I think of my room at Shoma's. How the tatami mats smell of grass. How I don't roll off the futon anymore while I sleep. The sounds of Shoma moving around the apartment in the middle of the night, trying to be quiet but not doing such a great job. I think of the neighborhood around his apartment, with its cafés and shops and konbinis.

I can navigate the streets now with my eyes closed.

I know its shortcuts by heart.

"Your friends from Vancouver can visit whenever they want," Shoma says. "Sometimes I'll have to be away for work, but it won't happen often." *And I'll always come back.* "Or I'll keep those to weekends, so you can just come with me. So what do you think?"

The idea of moving back to Tokyo and living with my brother—I already know I want to say yes. My heart hurts with wanting to say yes.

I'll miss Vancouver. I'll miss Gemma and Jory, my old house. I'll even miss Grandpa, the small peeks of his personality I was beginning to know. All those things—I'll keep some of them with me.

And what it's really about is this:

I think I owe Shoma a chance to learn about family again.

I'd want that same chance, if he were the one visiting me, and he was figuring out what home really meant, and wondering if he should stay.

I'm even thinking about our dad. I want to ask him about work. To hear him tell me how it means everything, to know that I'm okay with it.

I owe myself that, too.

"You don't have to decide now." Shoma peers up at the oversized clock on the wall—I have to go. "It'll probably take a few weeks to organize all the paperwork, anyway. Maybe you can think about it and—"

"I already have." I rush toward the doors—it's no longer hard to leave because the faster I'm gone, the faster I can be back—and call out one more thing. "But can you start keeping real food in the house?"

My brother's smile is as big as mine. He gives me a wave. "Sounds good."

I wave back, and then I'm in security, dropping my backpack onto the moving belt. I pick it up on the other side of the scanner and practically sprint toward my assigned gate. The whole time I'm still grinning, unable to stop.

Coming here for the summer, it wasn't because Tokyo was supposed to be a new home, even if I hadn't exactly been sad leaving Vancouver. While flying over the ocean, I'd spent the hours going back and forth, so unsure—which place felt less wrong for me?

I hadn't guessed it would end up that both were *right*, each in their own way.

So now I know it's not about roots only growing deep. They can grow outward, too, toward people, and places, a feeling.

That's home.

You take it with you.

ACKNOWLEDGMENTS

This book is so very special to me, and it's a dream come true to now have it out in the world. But I didn't do it alone and without a lot of help along the way.

My most heartfelt thanks to my wonderful agent, Victoria Marini, who got this book from the very start, who wields magic behind the scenes, who makes it all happen. Thank you forever and ever, Victoria.

Countless thank-yous to my amazing editor, Anna Roberto, for embracing this book as fully as she did and for her guidance in helping me make it shine as brightly as possible. Anna, it's been nothing but a joy to work with you.

So many thanks to in-house designer Carol Ly, production editor Alexei Esikoff, production manager Kim Waymer, copyeditor Jill Amack, and everyone else at Feiwel & Friends for being an incredible publishing home.

To the stunningly talented Lynn Scurfield, thank you for so generously sharing with me your gorgeous artwork. You've brought Kaede and his story to life in yet another way, and I couldn't have asked for a more perfect book cover.

Tons of thanks to my early readers Alyssa Keiko, Matthew Ringler, Ellen Oh, Emma Pass, and Kimberly Ito—your feedback was immensely valuable, and I'll always be grateful for your time and thoughtfulness.

To family, lots more thank-yous. Special shout-outs to my dad, Bak Wong, whom I miss very, very much. Thanks for all those thousands of trips to the library when I was kid—I wish we could go together one more time. My mom, Hing Wong, for being the very first person to tell me I should write stories for a living. My sister, Wendy Wong, who owes me a concert next time she's in town. And to Jesse, Matthew, and Gillian—thank you so much for helping me fill this book with our time together here in Japan. You guys will always be everything.

Also, this book wouldn't exist if not for Nothing's Carved In Stone and their music. Thank you for your songs, your shows, and for inspiring me to write *All the Ways Home*. I had the absolute best time doing so.

Thank you for reading this Feiwel and Friends book.
The Friends who made

ALL THE WAYS HOME

possible are:

JEAN FEIWEL
PUBLISHER

LIZ SZABLA
ASSOCIATE PUBLISHER

RICH DEAS
SENIOR CREATIVE DIRECTOR

HOLLY WEST
SENIOR EDITOR

ALEXEI ESIKOFF
SENIOR MANAGING EDITOR

KIM WAYMER
SENIOR PRODUCTION MANAGER

ANNA ROBERTO
SENIOR EDITOR

VAL OTAROD
ASSOCIATE EDITOR

KAT BRZOZOWSKI
SENIOR EDITOR

ANNA POON
ASSISTANT EDITOR

EMILY SETTLE
ASSOCIATE EDITOR

CAROL LY
SENIOR DESIGNER

Follow us on Facebook or visit us online at mackids.com.
OUR BOOKS ARE FRIENDS FOR LIFE